It Emptied Us:
From Tragedy to Forgiveness

Rick Collins

Rick Collins

Printed in the United States of America

First Printing, 2019

ISBN:
9781098923754

DEDICATION

I dedicate this book to my wife, Betsy Collins. I am because she is.

Rick Collins

CONTENTS

ACKNOWLEDGMENTS

I want to acknowledge the hard work and dedication of Vangella Buchanan. Without her guidance and experience, I would not have been able to finish what I set out to do. I also want to acknowledge my dear friend, Douglas Haddad. He believed in me and motivated me with his kind and constant support and encouragement. Finally, I want to thank all of the teachers, coaches, and friends from my hometown of Andover, Massachusetts. What a wonderful place to grow.

Rick Collins

Chapter 1

Broken Glass

"We have to leave," Donna Wilson yelled from the bedroom. "We don't have time!"

Donna's mother, Gwen, sat on a chair in the kitchen, rocking her twelve-year-old son, Bobby. His beautiful blond hair was plastered with blood and his elbows were cut and bruised. He was Donna's twin, but right now, he was very much a little boy. Bobby stopped crying and pulled himself up. His sister's voice was urgent.

"I called Aunt Carole! She's coming now. She'll get us to the bus station."

"Go, Bobby," Gwen urged. "Get some things. Put them in your duffle bag. We're leaving."

Gwen gently moved her son toward his room. He stepped over broken plates and some smashed glasses. He moved past the stove and stepped over the frying pan and the dinner that littered the floor. He slipped on some blood, but he caught himself before he could fall; the jolt of it sent him in tears again. Bobby stepped toward his room door and used his special key to unlock it. The lock clicked and he pushed the door open. He pulled a duffel bag from his closet and stuffed in some jeans, t-shirts, socks, and underwear. He grabbed a Cleveland Brown's football jacket and a Jim Brown Bobble Head before he turned to leave the room. The family picture on top of his clothes drawer caught his attention. He picked it up and held it for a moment. He looked at the faces of a perfect family and a rage surged through him. He pulled back his fist and smashed it against the glass surface. Shards of glass crashed against his bedroom wall. Blood flowed from his knuckles. He threw his bedroom key on the floor and walked out. His crying was over.

Bobby's twin, Donna, helped her mom pack. She stuffed clothes and toiletries into an old green suitcase, the one her mom was given as a wedding present back when her husband seemed to love her and he had a steady job and he didn't drink so much. Donna felt the back of her head. A clump of hair was matted down with blood. She had bruises on the palms of both hands. She pulled out a card from the back of her jeans. *Youngstown Police: To Protect and to Serve.* On it were the name and number of the officer who talked with her before she left the police station. She wrapped her fingers around the card, and crumpled it. She walked to the bathroom and dropped it into the toilet and flushed. The water made a gurgle and Donna watched the card disappear and get swallowed into the pipes.

Gwen stood up and crammed clothes into the suitcase. She bumped her arm into her bed stand and a shot of pain blazed through her bicep and into her shoulder. She dropped a sweater. She stooped to retrieve it and more pain rippled through her back. She tried to use her good arm to rub the deep, black bruise, but it didn't help much.

Donna heard tires on the gravel driveway. She quickly grabbed her mother's suitcase in one hand and hers in the other.

"She's here! Let's go."

Donna hurried her mother and brother out the front door. Gwen's sister, Carole, ran to hug first Gwen, then Bobby, then Donna.

"My God! Oh, my God. Get in the car. Quick, get in the car." Tears streamed down her face as Carole took the suitcases and put them in the trunk of her old faded-green Chevy. She ran back and jumped in the waiting car. Donna got to ride shotgun. Bobby carefully helped his mother into the back seat. He buckled her seatbelt and slid in beside her and held onto her. The blood had dried in his golden hair.

Carole put the car in reverse and backed out of the driveway. She threw the car into first and accelerated down the state road. The car bucked when she tried to kick it into second, and jostled Donna and Bobby and Gwen. Carole glanced in the rear-view mirror and saw her sister wince. Gwen had a black eye and a swollen jaw. Carole watched Bobby as he held his mother. If it wasn't so horrible, they both would have looked sweet.

The State road led back to town. To get to the bus station, Carole drove past the GM plant where they made the Buicks and the Chevys and the Cadillacs. She slowed and passed the police station. She held her breath, and the station disappeared behind her. She knew her sister's husband was deep inside that place and she knew he was going to be released soon. He always got released. She gripped the steering wheel and tried to keep a steady pace until she entered the center of town.

The bus station was run down, even for Youngstown. A guy in a glass booth sold tickets. Carole pulled the car into a parking slot and helped her sister and her niece and nephew take their bags and they sat in a darkened part of the station. They smelled diesel fumes and years of dust. Carole went to the ticket guy and bought three one-way tickets. She looked around to make sure no one watched. Faceless people walked and took no notice. A bus pulled into the station and people got off. They moved off and went where they were going to go. A bus driver with the name "Stan" sewed on his shirt pocket stepped down the stairs and went to relieve himself. His shirt was dotted with food stains. A gust of wind swirled some wrappers into the air and threw them nowhere. It was a hot day. A threat of a thunderstorm was in the air and the sky looked green. Gwen felt sweat roll down her back.

"I got you three tickets." Carole pointed to the same bus that had just pulled in. "That bus is going to St. Louis first, then down to Memphis, then Tulsa, and Phoenix, and then to Bakersfield."

"That's so far," Donna whispered. "I'll be so far from you."

"It has to be far away," Carole continued. "Anyway, when you get to Bakersfield, you call. Tell me where, and I'll send you money. I don't have much, but it'll have to do." Carole pulled her sister up and hugged her. "You have to leave here. You'll die in this place. You know that."

Donna stood up and took her mom's hands.

"She's right, mom. We have to go."

She picked up the suitcases and Bobby grabbed his duffle bag. Carole hugged them both. She looked deep into Bobby's eyes.

"You did right by your mom. Never forget that."

She kissed him first on one cheek and then the other. She wet her fingers and tried to clean some of the blood from Bobby's hair. She worked at it, but the blood was dry and wouldn't wash out. People boarded the bus. The driver came back with a Coke and a burger. He didn't have a napkin.

"Get on the bus, Gwen."

Carole gestured to the bus and Gwen Wilson and her twin children stepped up the steps and walked toward the back and sat by themselves. They held their luggage close. The driver started the bus and the air brakes hissed. He pulled the bus out of the station and drove it down the road past the police station. Gwen looked at the station through the dirty bus window and she wished the bus would drive faster. Her husband was in there and she wanted to be gone.

The bus drove past the car factories with broken windows and the mills with mostly empty parking lots and past the dry cornfields and finally past their old house. Gwen and Donna and Bobby looked at their old house one more time. The bus drove on. They turned their faces away for the last time and they traveled west and did not look back. The thunderstorm broke and rain fell hard and cleaned the town of most of its sins.

Chapter 2

Fumbles

Tim placed his hands under center. He was nine years old and the quarterback of the "B" team Beaumont, Massachusetts Chargers. He looked across at the other team and saw the eyes of his best friend, Andy Jones, linebacker for the rival Central Colts. Andy's eyes smoldered as Tim readied for the snap. He was intent on one thing, best friend or no best friend. He was going to sack Tim. And Tim knew it. Tim's dad, Coach Joe of the Beaumont High School Warriors, watched from the sideline. He kept his distance from the other fathers. He stood motionless, like a statue of some war hero. If he was nervous like his son, it didn't show.

Tim called out the cadence in his high-pitched, nine-year-old voice. This was supposed to be a pass play and Tim was ready to show off his arm. He knew exactly who was going to catch his pass. Jeff Tony, the team split end, readied himself as the ball was snapped. Jeff bolted, raced in an arc toward the sideline, and flew downfield. He looked back and expected to see Tim's pass, except, no pass came. A pile of black and white jerseys piled onto a lone blue and gold figure. The snap was perfect, but Tim pulled his hands out too quickly. The pigskin plopped onto the muddy turf. Tim pounced, panic in his eyes. Too late. Andy saw the bad handoff and leaped onto the ball. He fought Tim until he wrestled the ball out of Tim's hands.

"My ball. My ball!" Andy hollered.

The referee untangled the pile and signaled, "First down, Colts!" Andy leaped up and held the ball skyward. The other Colt players leaped in celebration.

The first play of the game was an utter disaster for Tim. He slowly pulled himself onto his knees. His hands were gummed with mud. His shoulders heaved and he cried within his helmet.

The cheers from the Colts knifed into Tim. He turned his head and looked to the sideline and he saw his father standing by himself away from the other parents.

"Get up, son."

Coach Joe saw the fumble. Everyone saw the fumble. The other fathers turned away quietly. They were glad it wasn't their kid who just fumbled on the very first play of the season.

So, "Get up, son," was all Tim heard, not in a booming voice, just simply, "Get up, son."

Tim pulled himself up. He wiped the mud from his hands and picked himself off the turf and looked at his father. Tim nodded once and turned away from the pile of Colt players. He jogged back to the sideline and bent over and tied his cleats. He stood back up and took a deep breath and let it out slowly, just like his dad taught him to do when things didn't go so well.

The Chargers never got back on offense. The Colts moved the ball deliberately down the field. Andy carried the ball on most plays. He never broke off a long run, but he simply would not go down. His older brothers, Zeke and Alex, members of the Colts "A" team and two years older, cheered each time Andy spun off a tackle, drove an extra yard, or fought for another inch.

Coach Joe watched Andy and the Colts move the ball down the field. Andy ground his way one last time for a touchdown. He hauled three Charger tacklers through the mud. Again, the referee yanked the Chargers off Andy, and again, Andy leaped up, this time with a scream of joy. His teammates mobbed him.

When the game ended, Tim and Coach Joe drove home. They had lived alone since when Tim turned three. Coach Joe looked at his son and wished she could have seen him grow up and hit baseballs and learn to read and skate and shoot baskets and catch fish. He wished she could have been at Tim's first communion or the day he broke his arm when he jumped off a swing or his first football practice and the day he tried on his football helmet to make sure it fit.

It had rained the night she packed and ran out in a downpour and jumped in a taxi and drove off and left them alone. He didn't know how to tell his son his mother left because she wanted more than a football coach and a little boy. Coach Joe ached at night when he rolled over on the bed they had shared and looked at the empty pillow where she used to rest her head.

He raised his son as best he could, and it was hard and football got in the way sometimes, so he brought Tim with him to every practice and game because he didn't know what else to do with a little boy. Tim picked up footballs and drank from the team water bucket and read books by the tackling dummies. The team helped Tim with his homework and talked about his day and told him stories about the things his father did at football practice and about their girlfriends and just about everything else that goes on with high school kids. Tim would stare at the players on his dad's team and he thought they were gods.

Tim would cry sometimes at night when he was a little boy and Coach Joe would go in and pick him up and sit with him in the rocking chair he bought for Tim's mom the day Tim was born. He'd tell Tim stories about football and growing up and being in the marines and getting his first job and moving to Beaumont. It helped calm Tim down and he would settle into his dad's lap and they would sing football fight songs and songs about being in the marines.

Coach Joe looked at Tim beside him in the car. His son rubbed some of the grass stain off his football pants and pushed his hair away from his eyes. Tim looked at his dad and squinted from the sunlight that glowed around his father. He rolled down the car window and put his hand out in the form of an airplane and flew it against the wind and Coach Joe drove the car and turned into the driveway of the same house he bought when he got married and things seemed simple.

The fumble never came up.

Chapter 3

Pistachios

After they stayed in Phoenix for a few weeks, the Wilsons packed up their meager belongings and took a bus west through Arizona and got off in Bakersfield, California. Gwen cabled her sister their location, and after renting a run-down apartment, the money arrived and she was able to move into an old, beaten-down house.

They ate little until Gwen found a job at the local pistachio plant. She woke up at 5:00 AM each day. She roused Donna and Bobby and made them breakfast. It wasn't much. They usually ate some cereal and maybe an English muffin and some milk. She helped the two get ready for school. Gwen took a shower when her kids were all set. When she finished her shower, she put on canvas overalls that seemed too heavy for the heat of the California desert, but she had to wear the heavy overalls since the pistachio plant was kept cold to keep the precious nuts from rotting. She kissed Bobby and Donna and walked out the door into the early morning California heat. She cooked in her heavy overalls and sat on a splintered bench and waited for the 7:00 a.m. bus. She climbed up the stairs and sat with other poor women and men who worked at the cold pistachio plant or the oven that was the pistachio fields. She sat across from many migrant farm workers who shared the bus with her. They talked quickly without looking at each other and she tried to understand their Spanish, but only caught a few words. She wondered what made them come to America. They looked at her and smiled and kept their own secrets.

Gwen worked twelve-hour shifts. Her overalls were soaked with sweat in spite of the refrigeration in the plant. She took the bus back home and walked the quarter mile to the house where she knew her children waited. When she got home, Bobby brought her a glass of warm water and a sandwich. He and Donna helped her take off her overalls until she was dressed only in drenched shorts and a t-shirt. Donna helped her mother into dry clothes and took her wet garments and the rest of their dirty clothes down the street to a local Laundromat. She did her homework there and waited for the clothes to come clean. She finished her school work and packed up the cleaned and dried old clothes and walked home in the dark.

Bobby pulled up a chair next to his mother and told her about his day. He told her about his math class and gym, and a teacher he didn't like very much. He told her about the kids from school and how they already had their friends and there was no room for him. He talked about the Mexican kids with their old shoes and dirty pants and matted down black hair. They usually sat away from him at lunch, so Bobby ate his bologna sandwiches by himself.

He told his mother he wanted to play football next year. He watched a practice after school and liked the way the guys hit each other.

"If your grades stay up."

Gwen reached over and brushed Bobby's gold hair away from his eyes. He sat crisscross on the floor and drank from an old glass. Donna came home from the Laundromat and the three of them read books and told stories and sang songs and stared out the window since they didn't have money for a TV. A lone fan pulled hot air in from the desert. Gwen got tired and Bobby and Donna helped her to bed. Bobby leaned over his mother and plumped her pillow and kissed her forehead and tried to smile. Donna laid out the overalls she cleaned earlier that night. She set out underwear and a t-shirt and some worn out shorts to go along with green work socks. She scrubbed the green pistachio from Gwen's shoes and dusted away the Bakersfield grit. She sat on the floor next to her mother and held her hand and sang a lullaby her mom used to sing when Donna was much younger. Gwen's eyes closed and she rolled over on her side and her breathing became quiet and peaceful. Donna saw bruises on her mother's lower back where there was a gap between her t-shirt and shorts. She gently pulled down the t-shirt so she wouldn't have to look at the black and blue welts any longer. She leaned over and kissed her mother's neck and brushed her hand through her mother's blond hair. She stood there for a moment, then walked to the door and closed it so it wouldn't make a sound.

Donna undressed and took a shower. She washed her gold hair with soap and tried to clean the dirt off her shins. She rubbed a bruise on her thigh from when she got kicked by some Bakersfield townie that played on the soccer team. Donna tried out as soon as the family got settled and she and Bobby enrolled in school. She was faster and stronger than the other girls on the team. This didn't make her any friends. They called her "hobo" behind her back or sometimes to her face. She decked the best girl on the team when they both fought for a header. The other girl slammed down on the ground and let out a groan and rolled over on her side and tried to get air back in her lungs and the girls on the team shut up. She walked home after that practice instead of taking the bus so she could calm down before she saw her brother and mother. She got home and helped Bobby sweep the house of the dirt and dust that couldn't be kept outside. She helped him with his homework and he helped her do the same. They sat side by side and finished their homework and waited for their mother to get home.

Donna and Bobby slept in the same bedroom. He was in bed when Donna finished her shower. She took a wet face cloth and put it on Bobby's forehead to keep him cool. She climbed onto her bed and pushed off the worn blanket and draped a face cloth over her eyes. Silver light from a full moon lit the Bakersfield night. A tiny sliver shined in through the lone window of their bedroom. They closed their eyes and listened to the sound coyotes made when they fought in the desert. Sometimes Bobby woke up from a terrible dream and Donna rocked her brother until he fell back to sleep. She held him and thought of Ohio and her dad and broken furniture and leaving on a bus she knew she and her brother and her mother had to take.

Chapter 4

Bigger and Stronger

Andy was bigger and stronger than Tim when they were in elementary school. But that changed miraculously the summer before Tim entered seventh grade and junior high. The coach of the West Beaumont Pop Warner football team was Coach Lou Sanoonian. He told Tim that he planned on turning him into a running back.

"You'd be good at it. Really good." He spat between chews on his old cigar. "It'd make your old man proud."

But Tim had no intention of playing Pop Warner again. His body began to change. The squeak in his voice was replaced by a deep rumble like a bass guitar. His legs and arms grew from skinny sinew to unexpected muscle. A couple years of weight lifting made an impact. Tim could no longer play baseball in his West Beaumont neighborhood. The second broken window of the neighbor's house proved that. And when he did play touch football with his pals, their hands throbbed after trying to catch Tim's bullet passes. When Tim ran the ball, no one could catch him. The few times Tim was cut off, he juked his buddies and raced away. Even though he loved Coach Sanoonian, Tim was going to make the West Junior High School seventh and eighth grade team. He was going to be their quarterback. And that was that.

Chapter 5

Hidden Bruises

Gwen Wilson sat in the employee lounge and drank water from a dented thermos. She opened a paper bag and took out a liverwurst sandwich. She took small bites between sips of water. She unbuttoned the top of her canvas overalls and let cool air flow in over her shoulders. Other workers sat about. Most had bag lunches. A few had lunch pails. A small, dark-skinned young woman sat alone on top of a pallet of pistachios. She ate some nuts and tried to be invisible. Gwen saw her each day, but the young woman spoke to no one. She unbuttoned her overalls and Gwen could see dark marks around the woman's neck and blue bruises on her left cheek.

The bruises on Gwen's neck and arms were mostly faded after a few months in Bakersfield, but she recognized the same marks on the dark-skinned young woman, and she recognized the way she pulled herself in and away from all the other workers at the pistachio plant.

Gwen remembered how she used to cover her swollen eyes with sunglasses and wore cheap scarves to hide the bruises on her neck. She remembered when she lived in Ohio and how sometimes coworkers stared because they didn't know what to say or do, and they'd go back to work and keep their backs turned until Gwen left the room. She remembered how she came home many times after work and put her kids in their bedrooms and waited for her husband and hoped his day at the Chevy plant went well. It seldom went well, and he'd come home, drink, get angry, and push her or slap her. Sometimes, he put his hands around her neck and shook her and pushed her and she'd crash into the kitchen table and Bobby would run out of his room and stand over his mother. His father would slap Bobby with the back of his hand or hit him with his heavy leather belt. Bobby stood like a stone and took the hits meant for his mother until his father got sick of beating him and went off and found a whiskey bottle and sat in his chair and drank and watched the game until he fell asleep.

Gwen took her sandwich and wrapped it back up. She walked over to the woman and squatted down so the two were at eye level. Gwen rested her hand on the dark woman's knee. It startled the woman and she recoiled. She pulled her legs up to her chest and wrapped her arms around her knees and squeezed herself in until she was a tiny ball.

"Honey? I'm sorry I startled you. I've seen you eat by yourself so I wanted to come over and share lunch. Would you mind if I sit with you?"

Gwen looked into the woman's eyes. The dark woman pulled her knees closer and gave a slight nod for Gwen to sit down.

Gwen sat and took out her sandwich and broke a piece off, offering her some. The dark woman slowly reached out and took the piece of the sandwich and took a small bite and then a bigger one until the sandwich disappeared. Gwen took out two apples and gave one to the woman.

"What's your name, honey? "

"Callista," the dark woman whispered and turned her head slowly to face Gwen.

She had jet black hair pulled back tight in a bun and smooth, dark skin that looked like the skin from a fifteen-year-old girl. Her eyes were deep brown chestnuts and her nose was small and bent a little bit to the left and her tiny fingers barely wrapped around the apple. Gwen watched the woman eat. She offered some water from her thermos and the woman took it and drank it until it was empty and she handed it back to Gwen.

"Gracias."

The dark, tiny woman pulled her feet under her knees. The sleeves of her overalls ran up her arms. Deep, black bruises showed against her brown skin and there were older scars on her forearms. Gwen took her hand and gently rubbed the dark woman's skin below the biggest bruise.

"Callista? What happened to you, honey?"

Callista pulled down her sleeves and slid away a bit on the pistachio pallet. Gwen sat for a while and then slid closer. She pulled up her own sleeves and put out her arms and showed Callista the deep, blue-green welt that had not fully healed from a night just a few months ago in Ohio. Callista let out a quick breath and looked back at Gwen.

"I do not know you. Why you show me this?"

"I have the same bruises as you. I'm safe here. So are my children. Are you safe? Do you live with someone, Callista?"

"*Si*. His name is Oscar. He pick pistachios."

Gwen sat closer and took Callista's other hand and gently pulled her close and looked into her eyes.

"Does Oscar hit you?"

Callista's chin dropped to her chest and a tear flowed down her dark face. It glowed from the lights high above her head in the rafters that held up the thin, metal roof of the factory. The dark woman shivered and tightened her overalls close to her chest and shoulders and took another bite of the apple and looked away and whispered to Gwen.

"Si. After work. He drink with his friends and come home late and he say he love me and then push me and hit me. I don't fight back. He too big and fat."

Gwen put down her sandwich bag and sat close to Callista and put her arm around her and rocked her back and forth and Callista tried to cry but could not do it anymore and workers picked up their lunch pails and shuffled back to work, and they left them alone.

"Do you have anywhere else to stay? Do you have any friends here?"

"No. Just Oscar."

The dark woman wiggled close to Gwen and tucked her head under Gwen's arm and used both tiny arms to pull Gwen in close. Gwen looked up at the lights in the rafters. She just found a job in Beaumont, Massachusetts and she was just about packed and would be leaving tomorrow with her twins. She looked at Callista and knew she probably had no other place to go and she knew Oscar would hit her again. She knew she could not save her. She leaned over and kissed Callista on the forehead and stood up and picked up her empty sandwich bag and the thermos and the old apple core. She buttoned her own overalls very tight and went back into the factory and put pistachios in bags and wondered if Callista would still be alive this time next year.

Chapter 6

The Jones Boys

The Beaumont High School Warriors played their first game of the season. Coach Joe was silent on the sideline as his team dismantled a very talented Lawrence High School Lancer team. The Lancers lost in the state semifinals last year. They returned half of their starters on offense and defense. They were the team to beat. Yet, here was Coach Joe and his Warriors knocking off the Lancers, 42-14. Coach Joe and the Lancer coach shook hands after the game.

"Fine game. You played well."

"Thanks, Coach Joe. I didn't think we'd lose tonight. Your team played better than we thought you could. Good luck the rest of the season."

The Lancer coach joined his team and they left the field. Beaumont was destined for another state title game. There was no team in the league that could stop the Warrior title train.

Andy and Tim waited at the gate as the victorious Warriors made their exit. They were immense in their mud-stained uniforms. They tousled Andy and Tim's hair and laughed with each other and jostled each other to get into the locker room. Andy and Tim dreamed of eye black smudged on their faces and bloody hands from fierce tackles and long, victorious battles in front of thousands. They dreamed of pride and honor and blue and gold uniforms and glory that would last forever.

Zeke and Alex appeared at the gate and stood next to their little brother. Both were stars of the Beaumont East Junior High team. The Jones boys' dad passed from a sudden heart attack a year ago. Coach Joe came to the Jones' house every night for weeks after the funeral. He'd climb the porch stairs and open the door and sit in the living room with the Jones boys and their mother, Mary. He'd talk about his day and they'd tell him about theirs. Sometimes he brought dinner and other times Mary and the Jones boys cooked. They'd clean up the table and wash the dishes and dry them and put them away together. He'd sit with Mary and hold her hand if she needed it or let her be if that was what she needed. He'd help Andy with writing assignments and Zeke with Algebra and Alex with Chemistry. When it was bedtime, Coach Joe let himself out. He'd come back the next evening for dinner, and every evening after that, until the three boys and their mother got back on their feet.

When all the players left the locker area, when all the parents and friends, the fans, the band and cheerleaders, when they all left, Coach Joe made his way toward his car. His son waited. Even the custodians had long since departed.

"Great game, Dad. Lawrence was a tough team. You handled them."

"The boys handled them."

That was all Coach Joe had to say, and he got in the car and so did Tim, and Tim began to understand what humility looked like.

Chapter 7

East and West

The next Thursday, the two junior highs, Beaumont West and Beaumont East, faced tough competition. East faced a very good Chelmsford squad. Early in the game, it was clear that Chelmsford was just too big and just too fast for Andy's East team. Although Chelmsford was clearly the better team, Andy and his teammates battled right to the end. On fourth and goal from the three-yard line, with East down 18-14, their quarterback tossed the ball to Andy. He was met immediately by two Chelmsford tacklers. Andy drove his knee high and extended a concrete stiff arm that sent both Chelmsford players crashing. The pylon was in sight. He dipped his shoulder and lunged for the goal line. An iron wall of Chelmsford defenders slammed Andy and drove him back just before he was about to score. Andy let out a grunt and his body was driven into the turf. The Chelmsford sideline leaped in celebration when the official marked the ball just short of the end zone. Andy lay on the ground. The ball rolled away from his grip. He stared into the sky and tried to focus his eyes. A few teammates helped their groggy star to the team bus.

"I should have made it in. I let you guys down," Andy said shakily.

His teammates helped him climb onto the bus and found him a seat and knew the game would have been a blowout if not for Andy Jones.

Meanwhile, the West Junior High Squad of seventh and eighth graders hosted Billerica. It was the second half when West's eighth grade starting quarterback, Daniel Russell, took the ball around his left end. The Billerica defense swarmed on top of Daniel. His body crumpled under the weight of the Billerica players and his ankle twisted awkwardly. The Billerica players celebrated while Daniel writhed on the ground. The trainer and the head coach raced onto the field. They checked his ankle and tried to get him to stand up, but it was clear that Daniel was done for the game. Two of the West players helped Daniel to the sideline. He could put no weight on his ankle and let out a curse when his leg grazed the ground.

"Tim. You're in," the coach called over to Tim.

He quickly buttoned his chin strap and raced onto the field. Daniel reached out a hand and Tim gave it a quick fist bump. He jogged to the huddle and called a play.

"Ok, slant pass, right. Ready, break!" The huddle broke off. Tim set up under center and called out the signals. "Popcorn 52, Popcorn, 52, ready, Go!" The ball was snapped and Tim kept his hands firmly against the center's backside. This time, on Tim's first play, the football did not come loose. He pulled the ball up to chest level and sprinted in an arc toward the sideline. His running back, Bill Bradner, angled toward the sideline seven yards down field, while the split end, Jeff Tony, ran a deep route. A defensive back raced toward Tim and leveled him with a wicked tackle, but not before Tim made the pass. Bill caught the ball and turned up field and raced down the sideline. Jeff Tony threw a great block and Bill sped past into the end zone. He held the ball high above his head and the entire West sideline erupted.

Tim did not see Bill score, but he did hear the crowd scream. He pulled himself up and saw cheerleaders dance and he shook some mud from his facemask and joined his teammates in the end zone. The West Beaumont eleven set up their huddle for the two-point conversion. Tim took the snap, faked to his fullback, Lou Zarro, and pitched the ball to Steve Staber, one of the team's best players. Tim was buried by a Billerica player and never saw Steve waltz into the end zone. Bill Bradner reached down to help Tim back to his feet.

"You're missing a great game lying face down on the ground."

"Thanks, Bill," Tim managed to say. He wiped another clump of mud from his facemask.

Tim made a touchdown saving tackle later in the game. He also picked off a deep pass and eluded three Billerica players on his way to a touchdown. Steve and Bill scored twice more and Lou Zarro roamed the field on defense like a madman.

Throughout the game, Coach Joe watched from the far sideline. When it ended, he walked to his car and started it up and drove away with one last look to the field where his son's team celebrated.

By the time they were freshmen, Tim and Andy were the best players in the league. They called each other often during the season. They ribbed each other about the long-anticipated game between East and West. West was 9-0 and East was 8-1. Tim's team already clinched the Valley freshman league title, but if East won, they would share the crown with West. That was very much East's intention, especially Andy Jones.

Alex and Zeke Jones played on Coach Joe's varsity. Their team was undefeated and headed to a state semi-final game in a few weeks, but the most important thing was the big game between both freshman teams just one day away. Side bets were made by the varsity players over who would win the East/West classic. There was still an intense rivalry between the East and West alumni. It was all in good fun. The varsity players had great memories of playing in the classic. For each classic, the whole town showed up. Part of the reason was Coach Joe. East and West had their own battered fields. By the end of the season, both fields were more dirt or mud than grass, so years ago, Coach Joe decided to move the game from one of the junior high fields to Memorial Field, home of the Beaumont Warrior varsity.

It was the dream for young boys in town to play in the game. When they were freshman, Zeke and Alex Jones led their East team to a come from behind victory over West. Both scored touchdowns late in the game to seal the win and hold bragging rights through their senior year.

The week of the classic, Tim and Andy did not talk to each other. They were best friends, and that might be forever, but not that week. The game was too important. Their friendship would have to wait.

Chapter 8

A Change at the Top

On Monday before the big game, Coach Lippman called the team together before practice.

"Gentlemen, I have someone I'd like you to meet. This is Bobby Wilson. His family just moved here from California. He has a twin sister, Donna, who will be on the soccer team. Bobby played ball in California. He's going to join the team this week. Please welcome him as part of West Junior High."

Tim sized Bobby up. Bobby was already over six feet and his long, blond hair hung down to his shoulders. Everyone on the team could see that Bobby was an athlete. His arms were already built. He had long, powerful legs and brilliant blue eyes to go along with his shimmering blond hair. Tim caught himself in a stare. He shook it off and walked up to Bobby's locker.

"Hey. I'm Tim. Welcome to the team. You timed it just right. This is the week we play East."

"Yeah, well, this isn't Californian football. But, sure. I'll play." Tim sensed the edge to Bobby's voice. The whole team did. But the kid looked like he could play.

"I'm a middle linebacker. I play fullback on offense. But middle linebacker's my thing." His blue eyes pierced Tim. "Yeah, I don't have to play fullback. Won't have time to learn the offense. Just put me on defense and get out of my way."

Tim was quiet for a moment.

"Like I said, I'm glad you're here."

Tim extended a hand. Bobby took it and put his full strength into the grip. It caught Tim off guard.

"Bring your best football to practice, Bobby."

"I'll bring it. Don't worry about that. See you on the field." Coach Lippman set up a locker for Bobby. He took his shirt off and the whole team noticed that, not only was Bobby built, he was jacked. He had ripped abs, bulging shoulders, and a man's chest. Tim swallowed hard and walked away and suited up and wondered what the hell just happened to his team.

Coach Lippman decided the team needed some extra tackling drills to get ready for East.

"You better stick Andy Jones and wrap him up. He never goes down on the first hit. We gang tackle, we win. You try solo tackles and Andy Jones will eat us up. He's one of the best backs this town has ever produced. It's going to take all of us working as a team to win this game."

"Who's this Andy Jones?"

Bobby grabbed Tim's shoulder and spun him around just before the tacking drill began. Tim stepped back and looked at Bobby.

"He's the best player for East. I've known him forever. He's my best friend, but not this week. We stop Andy, we win, just like Coach says."

"We'll see about this Andy Jones."

And with that, Bobby lined up in the tackling drill opposite Jeff Tony. Coach Lippman called everyone to attention.

"Ok, gentlemen, this is a drill. Tacklers, let up as you are about to make contact. Wide base, eyes up, wrap your arms, drive your legs. Bobby? Jeff? Ready?" Coach Lippman placed the whistle between his lips.

"Ready, coach," Jeff shouted.

Bobby said nothing. He set himself in a perfect linebacker stance, shoulders squared toward Jeff, hands on his knees. Coach Lippman blew his whistle and Jeff and Bobby raced towards each other. Jeff held the football firmly under his left armpit. Bobby covered the distance in surprising speed and drove his shoulder pads into Jeff's chest. Bobby drove his legs and wrapped his bulging arms around Jeff's lower back and lifted him a full foot off the ground. Bobby kept driving and lowered his center of gravity and pummeled Jeff into the turf. The air in Jeff's lungs burst out with a yelp as Bobby rolled off. He gathered himself and leaped up and ran back to the drill and cut off the next guy in line.

"What the hell?" Jeff cried, desperately trying to get air back into his lungs. "It's a freaking drill. You heard what coach said."

"Get up and let's do it again. I can do this all day."

Bobby turned his head from player to player.

"Anyone else?"

His eyes settled on Tim.

"What about you? Want to give me a try?"

Tim met Bobby's eyes with a glare of his own. He wasn't about to back out of a challenge, especially from a guy who just leveled his buddy.

"Ok, Wilson, let's go." Tim took the ball from Jeff who by now had regained his breath. "I'm ready. Blow the whistle, coach."

"Gentlemen, it's just a drill. Please remember that."

He raised the whistle to his lips. The piercing sound was magnified by the silence from the rest of the team.

Tim and Bobby hurtled toward each other. Time slowed, like a lightning bolt moments before the air splits. The collision was a thunder crash. Bobby drove his shoulder pads into Tim's chest. Tim's knees drove furiously into Bobby's gut. The girls' and boys' soccer teams heard the collision and they all stopped to watch. Teachers looked on from their cars in the parking lot and kids on buses stared out windows and grounds crew workers stopped cutting grass. Coach Lippman wedged between the combatants and shoved them apart, but not before Bobby threw a haymaker punch. His fist somehow found the space between Tim's face mask. It landed full on Tim's nose. Tim twisted and knocked Bobby's fist away. A streak of blood dripped down Bobby's knuckles. He bellowed at Tim.

"That's California football. Every play's a war. Get used to it!"

"Now you see what Beaumont football's all about. Don't ever try to take out a teammate of mine again. Ever!"

Tim tried to get at Bobby, but Jeff held him back. He tried to calm everyone down.

"It's cool. No harm done. Take it easy, Tim. California here was just showing us his game. Right, California?"

Jeff eased off his bear hug. Tim's breathing began to relax. Blood from his nose trickled to his mouth. He tasted it and spat.

"Save it for the game, if you get in against East. Just save it."

Tim backed off and let the football drop and it rolled toward Bobby. Bobby kicked it soccer style and it sailed off toward the girls' soccer field where his sister stood and watched.

"Oh, I am playing against East. Count on it. They better be ready for me."

Spit from Bobby's mouth shot out as he paced back and forth. The remainder of the West team gave him space. They didn't want to mess with this wild animal.

"You mean they better be ready for us," Tim countered.

Coach Lippman held up two hands in a stop sign.

"That's enough from both of you. Bobby, I decide who plays and who sits. You're new here, so now you understand. We win as a team, lose as a team. East/West is the biggest game of the season. You have to earn the honor of playing in this game."

Coach Lippman stood face to face with Bobby.

"Coach, I think I just earned some playing time."

He met Coach Lippmann's stare.

"We'll see, Bobby. Now, everyone, let's work on our plays for East. Let's go!"

Coach Lippman shouted and the team ran to the middle of the field. Bobby jogged behind. The knuckles on his left fist bled from the punch he threw at Tim.

Chapter 9

Fire and Ice

During English class, Tim took his normal seat, 2nd row by the window. His favorite teacher, Mr. Kennedy, worked with the class on Symbolism. Tim touched his black and blue nose and remembered Bobby's sucker punch and thought he understood Mr. Kennedy's lesson perfectly.

Tim took notes until he heard the door open. He glanced up, and for a moment, Tim thought Bobby had joined the class. But this was a girl. She walked in and Tim caught himself staring at her blond hair. Then Tim remembered Coach Lippmann mentioned that Bobby had a twin sister who played on the soccer team. This had to be her, so completely did she resemble Bobby. Minus the scowl.

"We have an addition to our English family. This is Donna Wilson. She moved in earlier this week, but only joins us today as she was helping her family get settled. Such is the character of the young woman we have before us, my dear students."

Mr. Kennedy made a flourish and Donna entered. Tim watched her move to an open seat at the other end of the class. She sat gracefully and didn't seem to have the nervousness of a new student or at least someone not used to moving. Mr. Kennedy handed her a copy of *A Song of Ice and Fire*.

"My dear, would you please consider the following passage? Let's put you directly in the fire, so to speak. What do you make of this?"

"When you play the game of thrones, you win or you die. There is no middle ground."

"Well, my lady. What say you?"

Donna read the passage to herself. Her eyes bore into the novel. The class waited. Perhaps this new student was not up to the task.

"I think. Well, I think we don't get to choose too often. Not our town, or our school, or our friends, or even our brothers. Not even our parents. And when we do get to choose, we either love them, or we don't. It's all of it or it's none of it."

The class was breathless. Mr. Kennedy looked at Donna for quite a while.

"Well, I suppose we shall let you stay, my lady. Thou has a lyrical heart, it would seem. Now, can anyone else match our new scholar in wit and understanding?"

No one moved. They were still too stunned by Donna's response, Tim not the least. And this was Bobby's twin?

When class ended, Tim moved toward the door to the hallway lockers. Donna stayed for a moment to speak with Mr. Kennedy about assignments she needed to complete. She turned as Tim was leaving.

"So, you're Tim. My brother told me about you. Said you were a bit of a dink."

She caught Tim completely off guard. First, why did Bobby bother to tell his sister about him, and how did Donna know she was talking to the same Tim? She smirked at him.

"He said he belted someone in the nose. I figured it was you."

"Yeah, well, it was a sucker punch. Maybe if I saw it coming."

"Take it easy, Beaumont boy. I'm just giving you a hard time. It's not the first sucker punch my brother has thrown, especially in football. He has a bit of an anger issue."

She held Tim's eyes. He found that he could not look away.

"He's just trying to make his mark." Tim tried to smile.

"You didn't just actually use a pun about my brother? Maybe you're not as stupid as he made you out to be."

To this, Tim had no answer. She moved past him into the hallway and Tim watched her walk away and he knew the hallway belonged to her now. She swayed as she walked and held her books just so and disappeared around a corner. Tim tried to catch his breath.

Chapter 10

The Classic

The crowd swelled to capacity as the East/West classic was about to begin. East came out in their white helmets, white visitor game shirts, and gold pants. West wore blue from head to toe. The only thing that both teams wore that was the same was a gold stripe, front to back, down the middle of their helmets.

To everyone in the stands, this would be a test of the will of two teams, led by their captains, Andy Jones for East and Coach Joe's son, Tim for West. Both players did not disappoint. Early in the game, Tim broke off a 70-yard touchdown run and then kicked his own extra point. Andy caught a pass and broke through two West defenders, including Tim, for a 30-yard score. Later, Tim picked off a pass intended for Andy and raced untouched for a 50-yard pick six. Andy stuffed Tim on a crucial third and short, jarred the ball loose, and scooped the ball up to score a 22-yard touchdown. Tim swayed on his knees and Andy celebrated. It was a bitter reminder of Tim and Andy's first football game against each other. Just like back when they were nine, Coach Joe stood silently on the sideline. This time, he did not need to encourage his son to get up. Tim pulled himself off the ground and jogged off the field to the encouragement of his teammates.

"We'll get it back," was all Tim said.

His teammates clapped him on the back.

Back and forth the battle raged. The West defense could not stop Andy Jones. Somehow, Andy turned certain losses into break away runs, mostly with Tim dragging Andy down from behind.

On a crucial third and four from the West 33-yard line, after another long drive highlighted by Andy, Coach Lippmann sent in a new player to spell one of his linebackers. The new player wore number 66. Gold hair streamed out from underneath his blue helmet.

"Number fifty, you're out. I'm taking your middle linebacker spot."

His hands dangled at his side and he bore his steely eyes across the field at Andy Jones. Bobby was sick of everyone saying how good Andy was, how he had to be stopped if West was going to win. He was done listening to that.

"They've got nothing!" Bobby yelled as the East quarterback was about to take the snap.

"Let's do this!" Tim yelled.

The ball was snapped and once again, the East quarterback pivoted and tossed the ball to Andy. This was another toss sweep, this time toward Tim's outside linebacker spot. He read the play and raced across the line of scrimmage. He barreled over an East player who tried to throw a block for Andy. Tim raced forward and immediately was eye to eye with his best friend. The collision sounded through the stadium as both warriors clashed. Tim had momentum as he plowed into Andy. He drove Andy back, expecting the referee to blow the whistle. And then Bobby collided with the two. He crashed through both Tim and Bobby and buried both of them into the sod. Coach Joe saw the crash. He didn't know for sure who Bobby was really tackling. During the hit, Andy's ankle bent over. He screamed in agony as Bobby jumped up and whooped with murderous glee. Tim rolled off his friend and knew immediately that Andy was hurt, and hurt badly. Tim took off his helmet and stood a few feet away as both the East and West coaches raced out to help. The varsity team doctor, there only to watch, rushed onto the field as well.

"Son, lay still. Let me have a look, please." The doctor's calmness stood in contrast to the utter horror of the crowd. It didn't matter now who won the game. One of their own was down.

"All right, this boy is going to need an ambulance. Coach Lippmann, can you signal the stretcher to be brought over. We're going to have to be careful to keep the ankle immobilized."

Coach Lippmann gestured to the nearby ambulance attendants and they hurriedly moved over the field with a mobile stretcher in tow. With the help of the doctor, they put a splint on Andy. He moaned in pain and slammed his right fist against the stretcher. Andy's two brothers, Zeke and Alex, came out of the stands and walked beside their brother as he was wheeled toward the ambulance. Each held one of Andy's hands. Coach Joe met Andy and his brothers at the ambulance. He looked deep into Andy's eyes.

"Sorry, Coach." Andy tried not to cry.

"Breathe, son. You'll be fine." Andy's labored breathing relaxed. "Take care of this one, Doc. He's a special young man."

The doctor and ambulance attendants made sure they did not jar Andy's ankle as they lifted him into the ambulance.

The East and West huddles were subdued. They watched their star and friend carted off and driven away in the ambulance. Both teams huddled for the next play.

"I got that sonofabitch!"

The West players were stunned to see Bobby sway back and forth like a wild creature. "I got him!" Bobby punched the air like he was hitting a prize fighter. Tim stared at Bobby and then lost it. He shoved Jeff Tony aside and jumped at Bobby and grabbed him under the armpits.

"Don't you ever, ever, celebrate after a kid gets hurt! Ever! Do you hear me?" He pulled down hard and jammed Bobby's face mask directly into his own.

"He'll be one of us next year!"

Tim held on to Bobby's armpits and Bobby tried to pull away. They would have thrown punches if there wasn't a game to finish.

Tim shoved Bobby and he stumbled backwards but regained his balance and looked like he was about to take a swing at the West captain. Jeff stepped in and pulled Tim away and the crowd watched in silence.

Coach Joe moved along the sideline. He saw the commotion in the West huddle. He saw Tim and Bobby mask to mask and he saw his son shove Bobby. Coach Joe chalked it up to the emotion of the game.

Donna and her mom watched from the West stands. Gwen Wilson didn't think her son would get into the game. Donna knew he would. Bobby wouldn't stand being left out of a game, never mind being on the team for less than a week without playing.

Donna remembered one football practice last year when they still lived in California. Bobby was an eighth grader playing on the freshman team. There was this time when during blocking drills, Bobby took a cheap shot at one of the older, bigger players. The kid challenged Bobby on the spot. Bobby told the kid to screw.

After practice, when her brother was by himself in the locker room, the same older kid from practice and two of his buddies walked in and cornered Bobby.

"That's the last time I'm taking cheap shots from you."

The older kid shoved Bobby against the metal lockers. His friends moved in. They reined blows against Bobby's face, shoulders, and back. Bobby managed to land a punch, but the freshmen were too big and too many. They left him bloody and bruised and curled up on the floor. Bobby lay there for a few minutes. When he felt like he could move, he picked himself up and crawled onto the bench in front of his locker. He tried to finish changing. He put one arm through his t-shirt and tried to pull the shirt down over his head, but it hurt too much so he took a deep breath and tried again and this time it popped through. He felt bile form in his throat and he swallowed and held it down and put his other arm through his shirt   He finished changing and limped out of the locker room.

Donna was there when Bobby came out of the locker room. She just finished her soccer practice. Two of the three players that beat Bobby waited for rides. Donna saw Bobby limp towards her. She hurried toward him and saw bruises and scratches on his face.

"Another fight? My God, Bobby." She carefully lifted his t-shirt to see deep bruises beginning to form on Bobby's ribs and side. "Who did this?"

"I'm fine. Leave it alone." Bobby pulled away from his sister. "Stay out of it." Donna looked at her brother and then looked around and saw two football players standing nearby. The grins on their faces turned to sneers.

"You did this."

Donna walked over to the first one. He laughed at her.

"Brother can't take care of himself," he said just before Donna kicked him in the nuts.

He collapsed in a heap and groaned and rolled up like a ball. Donna stood over him and glared down. The other guy stepped forward.
"Hey!"

He put a hand on Donna's shoulder and tried to turn her around. Instead, he was met with a full elbow to his face. He dropped to the ground with his buddy. Donna stood back and rubbed her elbow. She sneered and hissed while the two boys rolled on the ground.

"Why'd you do that? I can take care of myself." Bobby stepped up to his sister and shoved her and she shoved him back. He stepped back and grunted and grabbed his backpack and threw over his shoulder. She stood next to him and grunted back and looked out at the street. Their mom pulled up in their rusted red station wagon. The twins got in the back seat. Gwen Wilson drove away and Bobby and Donna sat as far away as possible and said nothing to each other. Gwen didn't notice that two boys tried to pick themselves up off the ground. The car drove off and the tailpipe belched smoke and the two boys coughed. One boy held his crotch while the other tried to stop the blood that oozed from his busted nose.

The Classic went on and Gwen watched her son shove back at one of his teammates in the West huddle. She took Donna's hand and squeezed it for the rest of the game. She saw Andy make one tackle where another East kid could not get up. The kid writhed on the ground while Bobby stood over him, feet planted defiantly on each side of the East player's waist. Gwen thought her son might reach down and pick the kid up and body-slam him again, but the East coaches ran over and Bobby finally stepped aside. An official pressed up against Bobby, nose to nose, and threatened him with a penalty, but Bobby stepped away and laughed at the official and jogged back to get ready for his next assault.

"My God. Donna, he's going to hurt someone. Look at him. He plays so angry."

"He is angry." Donna put her arm around her mother's shoulders. "It's been hard for him since Ohio."

"I know it has. It's been hard on all of us."

Gwen and Donna kept their arms around each other. The day was cold and small pellets of sleet fell from the darkened sky.

West went on to beat East by two touchdowns. Jeff Tony ran a bootleg play and scored from 40 yards out, and Tim ended another East drive with a diving interception along the sideline, right at the feet of Coach Joe. The game ended and the West kids mobbed each other at the middle of the field. The East kids huddled on their own sideline and tried not to look defeated. Bobby stood off by himself. His helmet was still buckled and his fists remained clenched.

Chapter 11

Quick Lou Zarro

That evening, Beaumont was set to play Chelmsford in a key league matchup. Early in the game, the connection between Zeke and Alex Jones seemed off. Zeke found Alex wide open on a number of plays, but either overthrew his brother or bounced balls at his feet. The few passes Zeke completed to Alex were quickly smothered by the Lions. It ended up taking monumental efforts from the rest of the team to pull off the win. The team was led by Daniel Russell, now playing split end opposite Alex, and the backfield trio of Steve Staber, Lou Zarro, and Bill Bradner. All three made key runs late in the game. Russell made a diving catch in the corner of the end zone. He cradled the ball in a magnificent one-handed catch.

The game ended with Beaumont on top, 26-22. Coach Joe breathed a sigh of relief and he left the field. The team changed in the locker room and left to meet friends and parents and the band and the cheerleaders. Steve , Bill, and Lou spoke to the press. Lou had been spectacular in the game. Bill and Steve taunted their friend.

"Quick, Lou! Let's go. We're hungry!" Steve beckoned to Lou.

"Quick Lou? Is that what the team calls you? Quick Lou Zarro?" A reporter made a note on his yellow pad.

"'Quick Lou!' I like the sound of that!" He jumped about and cackled the name, "Quick Lou!" His friends grabbed him by the arms and dragged him away and the three ran off and hollered, "Quick Lou Zarro!"

Coach Joe came out last. He wore dress clothes as he walked to the parking lot. His son waited for his dad at the car.

"The backfield played great. They really picked the team up with Zeke and Alex a bit off their game."

"Thank you, son. I'm heading to the hospital. Care to join me?"

"Yes. I want to make sure Andy's Ok, that he didn't think I tried to hurt him."

"Those things happen in games. It was just bad luck." Tim buckled up in the car beside his dad. He kept the huddle incident with Bobby to himself.

"Coach! Thanks for coming. I think I'm all right." Andy sat up in the hospital bed. Zeke and Alex sat on the far side of the room and wolfed down pizza and Gatorade. Their mom stood at the foot of Andy's bed. She had been to the hospital with her sons before. One time on the day her husband died.

"Coach Joe! You must be worn out after the game. You didn't need to come over." She took his hand and shook it and smiled kindly at him.

"It's all right, Mary."

The Jones brothers stood when Coach Joe entered the room. Tim was tucked behind his dad.

"You ok, son? I saw the tackle." Coach Joe moved to Andy's side.

"Yes, thank you, Coach. Doctors said it is just a high ankle sprain. They're letting me out tonight. They wanted to get the swelling down first." Andy's ankle was propped up on pillows. It was bound by ice packs and athletic tape. His brothers showed no mercy.

"You wuss! People across town could hear that yelp. You're fine!" Zeke tousled his little brother's hair.

"Didn't feel like coming to our game tonight? Took the night off, did ya?" Alex let out a Gatorade and pepperoni belch.

"Oh, sorry Coach." Alex apologized to Coach Joe. A gentle smile formed on his face.

"Why don't you gentleman get this young man and his mom home." Tim moved around from behind his dad.

"Andy, I'm sorry about the ankle. You were having a great game." Andy smiled when he saw his friend.

"You didn't mean it. It's just part of the game. Who was the other guy? The guy with the hair."

"Bobby Wilson. He just joined the team this week. From California."

"Tell him that was a hell of a hit. Good, clean football."

"Sure."

Tim looked down at the hospital floor. Coach Joe extended his hand and Andy shook it.

"Son, you get better. Let's go, Tim?"

The two left Andy with his brothers and mother. Tim and Coach Joe walked out into the dark parking lot and they got in the car and drove off.

Chapter 12

Thunderbolt

That Saturday night after the East/West classic and Beaumont's tough win over Chelmsford, Jeff Tony had a bunch of friends over his house. It wasn't exactly a party. Jeff's friends, including Tim and the rest of the West Beaumont football team, remained innocent when it came to parties and drinking. Jeff and Tim made a pledge to stay clean through high school. Other members of the team took the same oath, including their friend, Ike Nesbit. Still, there were the normal freshman activities. An occasional couple necked on the couch or kissed awkwardly in the game room. Tim watched in amusement.

"There goes Ike with Tammy, again."

Tim tapped Jeff on the shoulder.

"I thought they broke up!" Jeff laughed.

"Yeah, I think they did. Last party."

Tim grinned with Jeff.

And then the air in the room was sucked out. Donna Wilson walked down the stairs. The basement was dark and the glow from upstairs framed her in a golden hue. Tim looked up. He felt shaky. Something like nausea. More like getting hit by lightning.

"Is that you, Tim?" Donna glided down the darkened stairwell. "Is this what you call a party? It's not like this in California."

Tim met her at the very last stair.

"It's kind of boring really, I guess."

"No, I didn't mean those parties were my scene. I just meant, literally, that parties here are not like parties in California. I hated the drinking and the drugs back there. This is kind of cool. Sober freshman. Who knew? Maybe you can get me a bottle of water or something."

Tim stared at her for way too long and then backed away and moved off like a puppy. He quickly returned with bottled water for Donna and a Coke for himself.

"Let's sit down. I stand around and someone might ask me to dance."

Donna pushed Tim toward an empty old sofa and the two of them dropped down. Tim made sure to keep plenty of distance. He was a bit of a coward when it came to girls. But this Donna. Jesus!

"Nice game the other day. You played well for a kid from Massachusetts. Not like California players, but not bad."

"Yeah. Thanks," was all Tim could mumble.

"You can't read me very well, can you? I'm just busting on you. You played well. No need to be so modest."

Donna elbowed Tim in the ribs.

"It was a good game. I'm not sure we would have won if Andy Jones hadn't wrecked his ankle."

"Oh, yes. That was the tackle my brother and you made. Thor made quite an entrance with that play."

"Thor?"

"My mom and I call him that. He thinks he's a Norse god. Acts like that at home. We put him in his place."

"He was a wild man."

Tim thought of himself yanking Bobby's facemask in the huddle.

"He's played angry like that since we moved to California from Ohio a few years ago."

"Why did you move?" Tim turned his body to face Donna.

"We just moved. My mom found a job here. That's it."

Tim sank deeper into the couch.

"What about your dad?" Tim asked.

She sat for a moment on the couch and looked at him for a while and then jammed her elbow in his ribs again. This time Tim yelped. She put her hand on Tim's shoulder.

"Hey, I didn't think I wanted to dance. Come on. I do now."

She grabbed Tim by the hands and yanked him up. She was way stronger than Tim expected. He stumbled and Donna had to catch him to keep him from falling. She put her arms around his shoulders and began to do this twist dance thing. He looked at her and tried to imitate her moves, but he didn't know how to dance so she took his hands and led him. It was a fast song, so no worries. A slow song and Tim knew he would be way, way over his head. Maybe he already was.

Chapter 13

Easties and Westies

Ike Nesbit planned to have a party for both the Eastie and Westie freshman at the end of the school year. They were going to join together as one class when they entered their sophomore year at Beaumont High. Ike thought it would be a good idea.

While the Westies were a bit naive about the rites of passage in Dover, the Easties were well versed. Tim heard about the Eastie parties, especially when he talked with Andy. There was plenty of drinking and smoking done by pretty much everyone from East, at least the way Andy told it. He drank a few beers here and there, but never to the point of getting wasted. But football, making the Beaumont Warrior Varsity team, and playing for Coach Joe, was everything to Tim and Andy. Both of them made a pact that they would skip right over the JV's that year and go straight to varsity. Beaumont made it to the state finals last year, only to come up short in an overtime loss to Catholic Memorial from Boston. But this year, both the Jones boys were back for their final season. They both accepted scholarships: Zeke From Rhode Island and Alex from UConn. They returned along with a massive offensive and defensive line. Bill Bradner, Steve Staber, and Lou Zarro were junior stars. Steve was being looked at by BC and Syracuse, while Bill already committed to play for Boston University. And Lou? All the New England schools were after him as well as a few of the bigger east coast schools like Clemson, and Miami.

Beaumont was loaded once again. Making the varsity team was a long shot for Andy and Tim. Bobby, on the other hand, was talked about as the next great middle linebacker to play for Coach Joe. He was a feared man. Everyone gave him space, even the older Jones brothers. Bobby was a shoe in, and he knew it.

The starters would be Zeke Jones at quarterback, with Daniel Russell at free safety and also as Zeke's backup at quarterback. Alex Jones had a lock on one split end position as well as cornerback. He was named All State the previous year by the Boston Globe. So that was that. The other split end position was up for grabs, with many juniors and seniors in competition. Daniel Russell had the best shot. Jeff Tony had an outside chance. Steve would play one running back spot and outside linebacker and Bill at the other running back and also play corner. Quick Lou would play fullback and anchor the defense as its nose guard. Even with the Jones boys, Zarro was probably the best player on the field. This left Andy as a possible backup to Lou Zarro at fullback, if Andy could make varsity. Tim hoped to make it as a sub for Staber and Bradner. He was just as fast as them, maybe even faster. But they were bigger and had varsity experience. It was a leap to play varsity as a sophomore. Tim knew it. He also knew that his dream of playing for his dad might be a bit of an issue. If he made the varsity, there might be whispers that he made the team because of his old man. All these thoughts crept into his mind of late, but tonight? Tonight was Ike's party, the first night where the Westies and Easties came together.

Jeff's mom dropped off he and Tim at the party. Ike's backyard was packed with kids. The smell of cigarettes filled the night. Tim saw that almost everyone he knew from West was already there. They hung out on one side of Ike's yard while many unfamiliar faces turned to face Tim and Joe from the other side. Most of the Easties had beers. Some smoked. There was also a new smell hanging about. Some of the Easties smoked joints. Tim and Joe exchanged glances as if to say, "What the hell have we gotten into?" but moved through the crowd toward the music blasting from two huge speakers. There was Ike, and he had a huge grin on his face and a beer in one hand and burger in the other. He had cases of beer at his feet and joyfully passed them out to anyone who asked. So much for the Westie pledge.

Rick Collins

"Gentlemen, ah gentlemen, here you go. Have yourselves a cold one. What a night!"

Ike handed two beers to Tim and Jeff.

"No thanks, Ike." Tim took the two beers and gave them to two Eastie girls. "What about the pledge?" Tim looked at his friend.

"It's a new year, boys. Stop being dramatic. You knew this night would come. Andy, Jeff, you take one."

Ike extended a beer to Jeff. He took it and then handed it back to Ike.

"I'll pass too, Ike. No thanks." Jeff shook his head as he and Tim moved off. They grabbed a burger and some water. "We'll be over there, Ike. Thanks for having us."

Tim waved back. Ike lifted a beer above his head and two Westie girls asked for beers and Ike obliged.

Tim and Jeff moved off, saying hello to their Westie friends. Some ate burgers or hot dogs, but a bunch drank beers and some of them smoked, probably for the first time. Jeff noticed a couple Westies huddled with some Easties. The smell of weed drifted through the party. It was kind of hard to ignore.

"What a scene!"

It was the unmistakable laughter of Andy Jones who grabbed Tim from behind and wrestled him to the ground. As he straddled Tim, Andy pounded him with fake punches. Jeff jumped on top of the two friends and tried to pry Andy off the helpless and hapless Tim. The three laughed in hysterics and Easties and Westies ran over to make a circle around the three. Laughter erupted from everyone when Tim jammed his right knee into Andy's crotch, just hard enough to make Andy roll off. Tim then jumped on Andy.

"Get off me, you bastard! You win, you win!" Tim rolled off and Andy and Jeff lay on the ground and the crowd smiled to see such great friends. It was the unofficial signal to everyone that the gap

46

between Eastie and Westie was bridged. Ike jacked up the rock music. Everyone leaped in unison to the blare of heavy metal. This was now the new sophomore class of Beaumont High School.

"Here we are! Three of the best football players this town has ever seen. Can't wait to play for the Warriors!"

Andy clapped Jeff and Tim on the back.

"Do you think we really have a shot to make varsity? Maybe you guys, but not me. There's too much talent. I'm too slow anyway." Jeff laughed. He knew he was a longshot. Still, one could hope.

"We all have a shot." Tim looked into Andy's green eyes. "What do you think?"

"Tonight, we're all on varsity. Party!"

Andy screamed and he dove into another pile of friends. He head-locked one Eastie guy and put his arm around a Westie girl. Tim and Jeff watched their friend and put their arms around each other. This was what it was going to be like for the next three years.

"So, are you going to get me a burger? How long do I have to stand here?"

Tim turned around, and in the dark he saw Donna Wilson walk toward him. She wore frayed, jean shorts and a blue and gold tank top. Her long blond hair was in a ponytail tucked through a Warrior soccer hat. Even though it was dark at the party, her eyes and smile lit the space around her with a golden glow. Tim felt the air leave his chest again, like it always did when she showed up. They became close friends during freshman year. Tim watched Donna play hockey for the West freshmen. She didn't so much skate on the ice. She glided around, past, and by would-be defenders. She scored almost at will, just like she did when she joined the soccer team when she moved in at the end of the fall season. Tim thought she was the best athlete in school.

Donna came to all Tim's basketball games in the winter and track meets in the spring. She cheered him on when he stole the ball for an easy basket or pulled away from the field at a track meet. They always seemed to be picked up from practice or games at exactly the same time. She teased him mercilessly, and Tim basically took it like a dope. Mrs. Wilson and Coach Joe would exchange glances as Tim and Donna jumped into their cars. But Donna and Tim were just friends. Most people thought of them as a couple, but Donna and Tim never held hands or never kissed. They glowed when they were near each other. Still, when they were together, the Westies, and now the Easties could see their connection. As for Tim, when he saw Donna, Jesus!

"Didn't see you there. You snuck up from behind, again. Why do you do that?" Tim laughed. His breathing began to **return to** normal.

"Because I know I can. It's fun to see you try to catch your breath. It's like you're all, 'What light in yonder window breaks?'"

She loved dropping Shakespeare on Tim since it clearly forced him to grope for some famous line, even if it didn't quite fit the conversation.

"Um, me thinks thou protest too much?" It was a lame attempt to keep up with Donna, and of course, Tim knew it. She laughed at him. Tim pushed her shoulder. "Alright. Alright! Enough. Do you want a burger or what?"

"Me thinks thou protest just enough. Lead on, fair Hamlet."

And the two made their way to the grill and grabbed a couple burgers. Tim put on a bit too much ketchup. Donna grabbed extra napkins and held them in front of Tim dramatically.

"I'm sure you'll need some of these."

She stuck the napkins in her jean shorts. It forced Tim to look down at Donna's long legs. God.

A commotion grew over by Ike. And there was Bobby. He raised a beer high over his head.

"Who wants another? What, do you think we're going to live forever?"

A bunch of kids rushed over, and soon, many of them downed beers with Bobby.

"I'll take one, you prick!"

Andy moved over to the commotion and the blaring music and the beers and Bobby. This was the first time the two had been together since the East/West classic. A few kids hesitated when Andy and Bobby stood and faced each other. Just about everyone remembered Andy being carted off after the vicious hit laid on him by Tim and Bobby. He tried to calm everyone down.

"Take it easy, everyone. I'm fine. It was a clean hit. It was a clean hit, wasn't it, Bobby?"

Both eyed each other like two prizefighters.

"Damn right it was a clean hit." Bobby stepped closer to Andy. It looked like he was about to draw blood. "Come here, you shit!" Bobby grabbed Andy and twisted him into a headlock. Surprisingly, Andy howled in laughter.

"All right, all right, enough, you dink!"

The two grabbed each other in a bear hug. The crowd let out their collective breath, as did Tim and Donna, especially Donna. She saw her twin brother act very differently when things got physical. She really never knew when her brother would pop. She saw him pop way too many times, playing sports, or in the hallways, or anywhere, really. She hated it. Especially back home in Ohio. But Bobby never popped at his sister, and he never, ever popped at his mom. Being in Massachusetts calmed her brother, although no one would have believed it.

"So, drink up! What the hell?"

Bobby grabbed another beer from Ike and shoved it at Andy. Andy screwed off the twist top and took a mighty gulp. "Now that's what I'm talking about. Again!" And Andy did.

They drank all night and soon were plastered. They ambled about Ike's backyard and jostled with new friends. They stumbled over to Donna and Tim. She took her hands out of her pockets and Tim wiped a bit of ketchup off his shirt.

"So Bobby, I see you've met Andy. Everything good between you two?"

Tim remembered the hit he and Bobby laid on Andy at the East/West classic. Tim didn't speak to Bobby after football season. Bobby went his own way and most times, Tim made sure to go in the opposite direction. Bobby spooked him. He saw Bobby pop a few times and it scared everyone involved. On one occasion, Tim stepped in to break up a fight. Bobby was pissed at some kid for bumping into him in the hallway and the kid mouthed off. Bobby busted the kid in the mouth and jumped on top and beat him with his elbows. Tim knew the kid who was being beaten and he jumped in and pulled Bobby off, but not before Bobby hit Tim with an elbow. It hit Tim in the jaw and he staggered back, but regained his balance and pulled Bobby away just before he jumped back on the bloodied kid. Bobby bristled to see his twin sister spend so much time with Tim, but he kept his distance and let his sister do whatever she wanted, even if it was to hang out with Tim the Prick, as Bobby liked to call him.

"Yeah, everything is freaking good. Ain't that right, Bobby?" Andy punched Bobby in the shoulder.

"Can't you see we're best friends now? Are you sure you don't want a beer, Donna?" Bobby extended a beer to his sister.

"I'm alright." Donna pushed the beer away. "Keep it under control, will you, Bobby?"

"Well, don't worry about us."

Bobby shoved his new friend back toward the party. Tim felt a twinge as his best friend moved off with Bobby.

"You and Andy are close." Donna saw the look in Tim's eyes. "Don't worry. Nothing can split friends apart."

Tim watched Andy meander off with Bobby and wondered if that was true.

Chapter 14

The Beaumont Varsity Warriors

Tryouts for the Beaumont Varsity Warrior football team came to an end. The sun baked the players and coaches at the last scrimmage. The starters, guys like Zeke and Alex Jones, Quick Lou, Bill Bradner, and Steve Staber finished their part of the scrimmage. They were clearly the best players on the field. Coach Joe watched quietly from the sidelines. He preferred to let his assistant coaches handle the scrimmage. Now it was time to step back and observe. He noticed everything. Extra blocks, swarming tackles, hustle plays. He noticed the guy who quit during a play and the guy who did not give up. He never missed anything when it came to his team and his boys. Some of his best players did not stand out initially. A slight nod of encouragement or a quiet word of praise set a fire in a young player. And Coach Joe was never negative. If a player messed up, Coach Joe saw it. But he said nothing. It would be later when he would place a hand on someone's shoulder pads and speak a word of encouragement.

Bobby played with the returning starters. Even as a sophomore, Bobby dominated on defense. He sacked Zeke viciously on one play. He hung on to Zeke's ankle, throwing the leg aside like a steak bone. He hauled down Bill Bradner from behind. Bobby's arms slid down to Bill's midsection and he held on with an iron grip. The team thought Bill died. He rolled on the ground in agony and wondered if he would be able to have children. The team howled. Bobby moved off. "Who's next?" That stopped the laughter.

Andy and Tim got their chance. Andy broke a tackle and drove fifteen yards for a first down. Tim took a swing pass and raced past everyone for a long touchdown, including Bobby. Tim felt

Bobby's hot breath right behind him. Tim tossed the ball to one of the assistant coaches.

"Prick," Tim heard Bobby mumble from behind.

Jeff Tony did not fare well. He dropped a sure pass from Daniel Russell and missed a block on one of Andy's runs. Still, he hustled everywhere and did make a nice catch toward the end of the scrimmage. He dove for the first down marker but came up short. Coach Joe watched Jeff's catch from the sideline.

Coach Joe called everyone into the gym when the scrimmage was done. This was the time for him to tell the team how many kids would make varsity. The magic number this year was 40. The team did the math. There were two slots for sophomores, and Bobby had one of those slots.

"I'll be meeting with all of you. You deserve that. Seniors, juniors, sophomores. No lists on a wall. I'll speak to each of you man to man." Tim and Andy sat upright. "OK. Take a shower. We'll call you in."

The assistant coaches herded the team to the locker room. Sweat hung off each player. Not all of it came from practice.

Each player spoke with Coach Joe. They appreciated his honesty. Kids who made JV were told what they needed to do to improve, but mostly, what they did well. Some were disappointed, but none felt slighted. They knew they would get their chance someday.

Bobby came out of Coach Joe's office. His expression was the same as always.

"Shit yeah, I made varsity. Damn right." He grabbed his clothes out of his locker and changed quickly and slammed the door shut. "Damn right!" He shoved past Tim who sat on the floor next to Andy.

Then Andy heard his name. He and Tim sat back to back in the corner of the locker room. Tim got up and extended a hand to help up his friend. Their eyes met.

"Good Luck."

"Thanks, Tim."

Andy moved hesitantly toward Coach Joe's office. A sophomore had three years to make varsity. Not Andy. This was it. To play with his brothers on the Warrior varsity, for Coach Joe. Damn. This was his moment and it scared the crap out of him.

Tim sat back down and splayed his legs on the floor. The locker area was empty. The thought burst into his mind that he held at bay all summer. "What if I do make the team?" Now that it came to the point, Tim was more afraid of making the team than being relegated to the JV. Would his teammates think he made the team because he was good, or because of his dad? It wasn't going to matter though. Andy was in Coach Joe's office for a long time, much longer than Bobby or the other players. He was excellent during practices and scrimmages over the last week. Tim could not envision Andy playing JV. He was just too good.

"Tim. Come on in."

It wasn't Coach Joe's voice. It was Andy's. Tim stood up and walked toward the door. Andy held it open. His face was serious, but still, there was a twinkle in Andy's eye. Tim walked in and felt like he was about to throw up.

"Close the door behind you."

Coach Joe motioned Tim to a chair. Surprisingly, Andy did not leave. He stood against the wall.

"As you know, the number of varsity players this year is 40. Andy makes 40."

"I understand, Coach. Andy earned the spot. You can't keep him off varsity." Tim's voice was shaky.

"Agreed. He's earned a spot. The problem is, he thinks the spot should go to you."

Tim sat dumbfounded. He looked up to his friend. The same serious face remained, but this time, Tim barely made out a sheepish grin on Andy's face. Coach Joe went on.

"Andy did something that should have gotten him kicked off the team. I can't believe it, really. He told me he wouldn't accept a varsity spot if you weren't given one as well." Andy shifted his weight. Now his face beamed. "So I suppose I can't move him to JV. He's too good. So I've agreed."

"Agreed to what?" Tim looked at his dad and then over to Andy.

"I'm giving a spot to you, too." Tim sat for a while and looked at his dad and then at Andy. He got up out of his chair and Andy reached out and shook Tim's hand.

"We've dreamed of this for years. We play together. Right, Coach?" Andy smiled widely.

"Don't give me a chance to change my mind. Get out, the both of you."

Coach Joe turned to paperwork on his desk. The two young men left the office. Tim closed the door carefully behind him.

"Are you kidding me?"

Tim grabbed Andy by the shoulders and shook him.

"We'll be champions together! Champions forever!" Andy yelled and he lifted Tim up and almost slammed his head into the ceiling."

"You sonofabitch!"

And the two hugged and danced around the lockers and didn't notice Coach Joe lock up and walk down the hallway.

Chapter 15

First Scores

It was another great season for Coach Joe and the Beaumont Warriors. They steam rolled their competition. Zeke and Alex left no doubt that they were two of the best football players in Massachusetts. Zeke threw 12 touchdown passes and amassed over 2000 yards in the air. Alex hauled in 8 of those touchdown passes and ran back two kickoffs for touchdowns. Quick Lou, Steve Staber, and Bill Bradner were the best Running Back trio in the state. They played exceptional defense. Staber and Bradner lead the conference in interceptions and Quick Lou Zarro couldn't be blocked. He led the state in sacks with 20, and tackles with 104.

Bobby was a madman. In one game, Bobby hit a player so hard the kid's helmet flew off and rolled across the field. The crowd thought there was a head still attached. The team doctor spent the rest of the game making sure the kid knew what day it was.

Beaumont took the field against a very talented Dracut Midshipmen team. They led Dracut 21-0 going into the fourth quarter. Tim and Andy saw limited action. Andy came in a few times to spell Quick Lou. Tim gave Bradner and Staber a breather here and there, but neither Andy nor Tim had been factors in the game. Both of them hoped they wouldn't screw up if they got in.

On a pass play late in the game, Daniel Russell was driven over backwards. He rolled over and yelped and grabbed his ankle. The team trainer came out and checked Daniel's ankle. Daniel got up and some teammates helped him to the sideline. Coach Joe walked over to the bench and put a hand on Daniel's shoulder pads and saw the exasperation in Daniel's eyes. Daniel ripped off his helmet and slammed it on the ground. An assistant coach nodded at Tim to go in for Daniel. Tim raced onto the field and into the defensive huddle. Zeke met him there.

"You got this. You've worked hard."

Zeke swatted Tim's helmet and broke the huddle and took his place at one of the corners. Tim moved deep to his free safety position. Dracut set up their offense. One of their running backs went in motion and created an overload on one side of the field. This left Bill one on one with Dracut's best receiver. One mistake and the Dracut kid would be wide open.

The center snapped the ball and the Dracut quarterback turned to hand it off to his running back. This sucked in all the linebackers. Bobby and Steve crashed into the Dracut running back and drove him deep into the turf before they realized they were faked out. There was no linebacker to help Bill. The Dracut receiver bolted off the line and headed in an arc toward the sideline. He hit the brakes and cut back over the middle of the field. The quarterback set his feet and made the pass just before he was buried by Quick Lou.

The Dracut kid had an easy score if he could just make the catch.

Donna sat in the stands with the rest of the sophomore girls. She saw Daniel get hurt and Tim take his place at safety.

Tim darted forward when he saw the ball leave the quarterback's hand. He zeroed in on the spot where the ball would meet the Dracut receiver. Just before the Dracut kid made the catch, Tim raced in front and plucked the ball out of the air and tucked it into his armpit and the crowd roared and Tim sprinted for the sideline. Steve and Bobby screamed, "Red! Red!" the signal that the pass was intercepted. Blue and gold uniforms turned and hunted down Dracut players.

Donna saw the interception about to take place. She felt the thrill before the rest of her friends. The entire Beaumont side of the stadium leapt while the Dracut fans groaned. Tim raced down the field with an escort of blue and gold uniforms. A lone Dracut player stood between Tim and a certain touchdown. She screamed, "Cut it back, Tim. Now!"

Two Beaumont players galloped ahead of Tim as the Dracut player made his move to make the tackle. Tim settled into third gear and let his teammates set up a block and Tim saw his chance. He cut hard to his right and broke into open field and his buddies plowed the Dracut kid into the ground. Tim shifted the football from one armpit to the other. He juked another Dracut player and raced for the end zone. He held the ball high above his head and the Beaumont fans went nuts.

Donna was swarmed by her friends. She never told them about how she felt about Tim, but they could see it. They noticed Donna's eyes linger just a bit too long on Tim when he left the lunchroom table, or when he always seemed to be the last guy to leave practice, usually the same time Donna just finished hers. If she wanted to keep that secret, it was fine with them. Secrets in a girl's heart are often hard to conceal. Donna saw Tim toss the ball to the official as his teammates mauled him in celebration. This time, it was Donna who felt the lightning bolt.

Chapter 16

Mary Jones and Gwen Wilson

The game ended and both teams filed out. The Beaumont band marched out of the stadium and played their victory song.

Gwen Wilson walked out with Mary Jones.

"Would you like to have a drink with me?" Mary put her arm around Gwen. "Let's get some pizza too."

"That would be lovely. Thank you, Mary."

Gwen and Mary walked out together and the crowd cheered and the band played and their sons showered and scrubbed off the grime from the game.

Mary and Gwen parked downtown at a place called "Mel's". They sat in an empty booth in a quiet corner of the restaurant. The waitress brought them beers and took their pizza order.

"Tell me about your husband, Mary."

Gwen put her beer down and looked at some of the other families in the restaurant. Mary picked up her beer and took a small sip. It took her some time before she replied.

"Gwen, it's been four years, and I swear to God I can still smell him on my pillow. We have an easy chair he used to sit in when he watched football games on TV with the boys. It still sags. I never got the chair fixed. I can't bring myself to do it."

The two sat in silence for a bit.

"I remember when he was in the hospital. The doctors said he needed a heart transplant. But we were pretty low on the list. A couple days later, he had another heart attack. This one was too big. I had the boys there to visit when the attack happened. They saw him turn blue. Having the boys see their father die almost killed me."

Gwen took Mary's hand.

"I'm so sorry."

She rubbed Mary's hand gently. Mary wept quietly in the dark. She took out a tissue and blew her nose and rolled it into a ball and pushed it aside. Slowly, her crying ebbed. She dabbed the remaining tears off her face and sat up straight.

"No, I'm sorry. I don't talk about him much, but when I think of him and the boys, it breaks my heart. They miss him. They don't talk to me about it, but I can see. They get really quiet sometimes. I give them space, and after a while, whatever pain they are feeling seems to pass."

"But what about you, Mary?" Gwen leaned closer. "What do you do when it hurts?

"I work. And watch the boys when they play football. I don't have anything else. I don't want anything else."

"I'm here for you, Mary."

Gwen got up and came around and sat down. She pulled Mary close. Mary started to cry again. The pizza arrived and the waiter put it on the table and gave them napkins and then left. Mary looked at her friend.

"What about you, Gwen? Why haven't you told me about your husband?"

Gwen left her arm around Mary's shoulder and sat a little while.

"It's a part of my life that I wish was over. I'm better now and so is Donna. She's doing great, actually. She's strong, Mary. So strong. She holds me together."

"What about Bobby?"

Mary took a sip of her beer and cut a small piece of pizza. She moved it to her mouth and ate it carefully. She wanted to make sure her mouth didn't get burned.

"Bobby hasn't let it go. He can't. It's eating him up, Mary. You see the way he plays. It scares me what he might do to someone on the field. I don't know if he'll ever heal."

Gwen looked at a family eating dinner at a table across the restaurant. The father cut spaghetti for his son and wiped off some sauce from his daughter's face. The mom smiled warmly and ate lasagna.

"What happened? Tell me."

Mary handed a slice of pizza to Gwen and looked at Gwen's arm. Old bruises were still there.

"Your husband. He hurt you, didn't he?"

Gwen looked away and spoke quietly.

"He hurt all of us."

"My God. I'm sorry, Gwen."

Gwen cried hard and they sat there for a while and didn't talk and drank some of their beers and moms and dads and kids came in and ate their dinners and left and got in their station wagons and drove away.

The game was over and the stands sat empty. Coach Joe turned the keys to lock up. A lone figure waited in the parking lot.

"Hey, Dad."

Tim slung his backpack over his shoulders. His hair dripped from the shower. A bit of eye black smudged his face.

"Good game, Tim."

Coach Joe shook his son's hand.

"Thanks, Coach."

They opened the car doors and buckled themselves in and Coach Joe turned the keys and put the car into drive. They drove home without speaking. Not every silence is awkward.

Chapter 17

In Your Face

Quick Lou Zarro had people over after the Dracut game. Steve Staber brought his girlfriend. They sat off in a dark part of the basement. Bill Bradner mingled with friends. He let out a full-throated laugh when one of his buddies cracked a joke. Daniel Russell stood with a couple girls. He was on crutches, again, and he was sick of it. Still, a part of him enjoyed the attention.

Jeff Tony saw no action during the game. He and Tim came to the party together and sat at a picnic table and ate hot dogs.

"I hoped I would get into the game today."

Jeff stood up glumly from the wood bench.

"You keep practicing your ass off. You'll get in."

Tim chomped on his hot dog and grinned at his friend.

"Everyone keeps talking about hustle plays, hustle plays. When does that pay off?"

This was delicate for Tim. Playing time was a Coach Joe decision. Tim was getting in games. One of his best friends wasn't.

"You're good. We've all seen it. I got in on defense. The game ended right after that. Maybe you would have gotten in if we got the ball back."

"Well, I didn't. I just want my chance."

Jeff picked up a water bottle and wandered off. Tim let him be.

The Jones boys arrived. The music seemed louder anytime the brothers were around. The entire school found themselves drawn to the Jones boys. The two seniors were surrounded by their friends while Andy made a beeline toward Tim.

"I told you we were going to be champions. What a freakin' awesome run, Tim. Awesome!!" This time it was Andy who lifted Tim up in the air. "The crowd went nuts. Your dad even cracked a smile. He tried not to, but I saw it. Coach Joe and his son!"

"Alright. Yeah, yeah, I got some good blocks. But thanks."

Tim playfully pushed Andy away.

"What, modest again? You know you love the attention!"

Donna appeared out of the dark like some spectral presence. Andy grinned from ear to ear as Donna moved up behind Tim and gave him a playful shove.

"Tim, the football star!"

"Come on. Easy, will you?"

It was a darkened room in Quick Lou's house, but everyone nearby saw Tim's blushing face. Andy certainly did.

"I'm off. Where's that dink Ike? Ike!"

And Andy moved away. Jeff stood nearby, but took the cue from Andy and walked out of the room. The guys in school saw the Donna/Tim thing develop, even if Tim was too stupid to see it for himself.

"You really did play great. That interception, my goodness!" Donna grabbed two sodas from an ice bucket and a bag of chips. She nudged Tim toward an open couch. It was more like a love seat. The two plopped down. Only then did Tim feel exhausted from the game. His calves ached and he had a welt on his shin.

"You look like crap, you know that? At least you showered. That would be too much, even for me."

"I am not an animal." He grinned and then found himself staring into Donna's eyes. "Damn. Give me some chips." She held his stare and handed him the chip bag. Tim felt himself dissolve.

"Heard you guys won your soccer game. What, like three goals for you? Again?"

Now it was Donna's turn to melt.

"You are something, Tim."

She nudged just a bit closer and took her closest leg and swung it over Tim's knee.

"Shut up or people might think I actually like you."

Donna fed him a chip. The kids at the party sensed Donna and Tim wanted to be alone so they moved off. Kids know stuff.

"I knew you were going to pick off that pass. Didn't think you had it in you to take it all the way for a touchdown, though."

She pressed her shoulder close to Tim. His damp hair dripped and some of it dropped onto her tank top.

"Dry off after a shower, maybe?" She moved close and her lips brushed Tim's. "Give me some of those chips."

He felt the lightning bolt again. He was getting used to it. He leaned closer, and this time the two kissed and held it, and were alone in space and they could hardly breathe.

Tim's collar was yanked and he was hauled off the couch. He lost his balance and crashed into the snack table.

"Keep away from my sister."

Bobby's chest heaved and he stepped between the couch and the sprawled Tim. His eyes were wild.

"Step off, Thor!"

Donna spun her brother and slid next to Tim who righted himself, ready to charge.

"This has nothing to do with you. Step off!"

Donna stood nose to nose with her brother. Bobby's breathing relaxed, but his eyes remained locked on Tim in a death stare.

"So now you know. You can't protect me forever. And there is no need for you to protect me from him."

She moved her arm through Tim's, and with her other hand punched her brother in the chest.

"You can't keep fighting battles that don't exist. Especially not here. You ass, you're safe. Bobby, don't you see that?"

"Fine. Pick who you want." His stare never left Tim. "I find out you hurt her, I will kill you. I don't care if Coach Joe is your dad." Bobby stormed off and grabbed a cup of beer and chugged it down and grabbed some friends and hauled them out of the basement. Donna pulled Tim back onto the couch. She picked some chips off the upholstery. She bit down on one of the chips and spit out a piece of dirt.

"You ok?"

Tim held Donna.

"I might be incorrect in my assessment, but I don't think your brother thinks highly of me."

"He doesn't hate you."

"So what is it? What did you mean, you're safe here?"

"Just that." Donna ate the rest of the chips without looking at Tim. "He can be a dick sometimes."

She put the bag of chips down and took Tim's hand in hers. Slowly the two of them began to hear the music again. She leaned her head against Tim's shoulder. They sat quietly. Once again, they became invisible to everyone but each other as the rock music thumped and the party room shrank.

Chapter 18

Hard Stuff

After Bobby left Donna and Tim, he strode through the basement of Quick Lou's house. He saw Andy and grabbed him and pushed him outside. Bobby pulled a bottle of vodka from the back pocket of his jeans. "We won. Drink!" He pushed the bottle at Andy. Andy drank beers at parties, not hard liquor, so he tried to hand it back.

"Don't be a pussy."

Bobby shoved the bottle back.

"I'm no pussy." Andy took a long pull from the bottle. His eyes bugged as he finished the swallow. He convulsed and coughed and let out a howl. "Jesus!" He felt a deep, hot burning down his throat as he tried to regain composure. "Damn!"

Bobby burst out in laughter and whacked his friend on the back.

"That's being a man. Give it back to me!"

Bobby ripped the bottle out of Andy's hands. Some of the booze splashed on them. Bobby reared back and finished the bottle.

"You're damn right. Another Warrior win!"

And he raised the bottle high into the night. He drank non-stop since he arrived at the party three hours earlier. He rocked forward and Andy caught him just before Bobby slammed into the side of Quick Lou's house. He held onto Andy and the backyard swirled. Andy saw tears slide down Bobby's face.

"What the hell? You crying? Jesus." Andy grabbed onto his friend and pulled him close. "What is it?"

"Screw football. Screw winning. And to hell with my old man." Bobby tried to pull away from Andy's grasp. "To hell with him."

Andy held on to Bobby who flailed his arms and kicked at the darkness.

"Screw who? Coach Joe?"

"No, no, no. Not him. Screw my old man."

"What about your old man?"

Andy tried to keep his senses as the three beers and hard swallow of vodka coursed through him. Bobby broke away from Andy and stumbled over to an old swing and sat down and pumped his legs. The swing creaked and Bobby swung in the darkness of the backyard. Finally, he jumped off and landed in saw dust. His momentum rocked him forward and he crashed hard on his face.

"Damn it."

Bobby sat up and tried one more time to suck any remaining vodka from the now empty bottle. He looked at it for a while and then threw the bottle deep into the nearby woods. It crashed against some unseen rock. The force of the throw knocked Bobby off balance again and he sprawled back on the ground. Sawdust stuck to his gold hair. Andy saw Bobby was about to pass out.

"Let's get you home. Sleep it off."

Andy put his arm around Bobby and picked him up and walked him to the front of the house where some kids passed around beers and joints.

"We need a ride!" Andy shouted.

Zeke and Alex were still there and helped both Andy and Bobby into their old, beaten truck. They started it up and drove off. Bobby's limp body pressed against Andy as the truck rolled through town. Andy ran his fingers through Bobby's hair. Bobby moaned a bit and quietly mumbled, "Stinking old man."

When they got to Bobby's house, Andy helped his drunk friend from the car. Bobby slurred, "Thang you, bud."

"Give me a minute. I'll be right back."

Zeke and Alex watched Andy shuffle Bobby through the front door. When Andy and Bobby got inside, Bobby's mom waited in the living room. She sat up from the couch and moved toward her son.

"Thank you for taking care of Bobby, Andy."

She took her son in her arms and helped him toward the stairs. She looked old in her brown work uniform.

As the two of them reached the top of the stairs, Andy saw Bobby's shoulders heave and he held on to his mother and cried and staggered.

"Screw dad."

Andy stepped away from the stairs and walked to the front door and opened it and walked out to his brother's truck.

"He looks hammered, Andy. He going to be ok?"

Zeke looked into Andy's eyes through the rear-view mirror. The way Andy looked reminded Zeke of the months after their father passed away.

"Let's get out of here."

Andy slumped in the back seat as the car moved down the driveway. He looked deep into the woods around Bobby's house and the darkness of the trees went on forever.

Chapter 19

Missing Mom

Steve drove Tim home from the party. He was thrilled that Tim played so well.

"You had a great game tonight. You might see more playing time if Daniel's ankle can't heal. Get yourself ready. Starting friggin' safety. I can't believe it!" Tim hopped out of the car.

"No, you played great, Steve. What, BC or Syracuse? Make up your mind yet? Tim looked through the driver's window at Steve. Aside from Tim's touchdown, Steve had scored all the rest. He had runs of 88 and 50 yards for scores, and took a pass over the middle from Zeke, broke two tackles and hauled another Dracut player into the end zone for his most impressive touchdown of the night.

"Hey, we have states to win this year, and next. College will take care of itself. But thanks."

Steve put the car into reverse. He straightened the car out and shifted to first gear and hit the gas and the tires squealed.

"Say goodnight to Coach Joe!" Tim heard Steve yell when his car reached the end of street. "States!" His voice faded into the darkness as Tim stood in the driveway with a smile on his face. He entered the darkened house and crept up to his room. A dim light was on in Coach Joe's bedroom. Tim knocked on the door and opened it and saw Coach Joe working on his plan for the next game. Tim took a chair next to his father's desk.

"Can't you take a night off? We just won."

"No. I can't." Coach Joe worked on some new play he had up his sleeve. Tim smiled as his father drew formations, blocking schemes, and pass patterns. Coach Joe put down his worn pencil and rubbed his temples.

"Did you have fun tonight?

"Yeah. I had a good time."

Where'd you go?"

"Out with some friends. Jeff Tony, Ike. We were over at Quick Lou's house."

"Just hanging out?"

"Yeah, just hanging out.

"Any drinking going on?" Tim sat still on the chair. "You know my rules. No drinking. No drugs."

"Not that I saw," Tim said quietly.

"We got states to win."

Coach Joe looked at his son.

"I was with Donna."

"Donna Wilson? Really? I like her."

"She's ok."

"You guys boyfriend and girlfriend?"

"No."

"Sure?"

"Yes. We're just friends, Ok?"

Tim's head drooped. His legs ached and he had a bruise on his ribs. After a moment, he looked up at his father.

"Do you think mom ever came to one of my games?"

Coach Joe picked his pencil back up and scribbled on the game-plan papers. Then he put it back down and adjusted his glasses and pinched his nose like it hurt. He held his breath for a second or two and let it out slowly.

"I think I saw her once at one of your junior high school football games. She stood next to a car in the parking lot of the school and watched you play. You scored on a long touchdown, and I glanced over and she made this small clapping motion with her hands. It was just a few claps, and then she put her hands over her mouth and held them there for a while. I took a step toward her from where I was standing on the field, but she put her hands down and hung her head and got in the car and drove off. She might have seen me. I don't know."

Tim looked at his dad.

"Football has been my life. It's the only thing I wanted to do or knew how to do. I think when I married your mom, she loved that about me. But I was who I was and I knew she was lonely. I spent hours in my office or watching film, and there wasn't a lot of room for her. We had you, and things got better for a while. But I coached and she left her job and took care of you, and I think she just wanted more."

"So, I wasn't enough for her?"

"No. I don't think that was it. She was a free spirit when I met her, and that's why I fell for her, but she was who she was, just like I was who I was. Sometimes, people can love each other and not be able to be with each other.

The night before she left, she held you in her rocking chair for hours and read you stories and played with your fingers and sang you songs. And when she was done, she came to bed and held me all night and never said a word. I knew I was about to lose her and I loved her so much, and when the next night came, it killed me to let her go. When you were younger, I sometimes hoped she would come back and everything would be fine, but she was dying inside, and I don't think it had anything to do with you and me."

Tim sat in his chair. He looked out the window of his dad's bedroom.

"You telling me this is supposed to make me understand, but I just don't. Jesus, dad, she was my mother and your wife."

"I know. Part of me hopes she's hurting as much as I hurt or you hurt. But I think that's me being selfish. I think she might have stayed if I begged her, but I knew, eventually, she would hate me for it, and maybe even hate you for it. I loved her enough to let her go and I have to think that it might have been the best thing for all of us."

Coach Joe picked up the pencil again and began to draw more X and O shapes. Tim got up from his chair and leaned over and kissed his father on the top of the head and turned around and walked to the door. He took hold of the knob and stepped out of the room and closed the door. He opened his bedroom door and lay down and looked at the ceiling and he thought about his father and what his mom might look like and he thought about Donna and Bobby and Andy's dad being gone. A lonely car drove pass his house, and after a while, Tim closed his eyes and hoped he wouldn't dream.

Chapter 20

States

Once again, the Beaumont Warriors dispatched all their league rivals, and after a hard-fought semi-final win over a strong Brockton Boxer's team, they reached yet another state championship; this time against the Salem Witches. Salem was undefeated and squashed their opponents from the Cape Ann League. In the state semi-finals, Salem knocked off a very talented team from Everette. It was the biggest upset in the state tournament. Everette rolled over their competition for years. Salem, somehow, hung around in the game, making the best of turnovers. They forced overtime, scoring on a great pass from their star quarterback, Jim Ryan, to maybe the second-best receiver in the state, Mike Sancouci. On fourth down, with Everette poised to tie the game, Sancouci drilled Everette's quarterback on a pass play. Ryan dove on the fumble and the upset was complete. Now Salem would face the Warriors in what promised to be the most exciting game in the state of Massachusetts.

The upcoming championship game consumed the town. Warrior banners flew proudly from downtown businesses and homes. Beaumont High School was apoplectic. The kids tried their best to stay focused on their classes, but even the teachers were distracted so that didn't help. Coach Joe had done it again, perhaps with his most talented team ever.

The teachers had the first opportunity to buy game tickets. They planned carpools for the game. Many of the players and cheerleaders and band members were their students. The coaches were their friends. It would be a day they would not forget.

The students scooped up the rest of the tickets. The high school included an extra two buck fee so buses could be rented to take the students to the game. Many of the kids organized their own rides, but still, 30 buses would be jammed with hysterical Warrior students. Noise makers were purchased. Banners were created by the pep squad and cheerleaders, and even the teachers bought replica team jerseys with names like Jones, Bradner, Zarro, and Staber.

Jeff Tony was given a varsity game shirt. He was going to be in the game. He got the news in a private meeting with Coach Joe.

"You've given the team your best all season. I'm sure you were frustrated that you didn't get to play with the varsity. But Jeff, we need you. We're moving you to varsity as our third string quarterback. Be ready. I believe in you, son."

Coach Joe handed Jeff a blue and gold jersey with the number 2 and his name, 'Tony" stitched perfectly on the back. Jeff found it hard to look into Coach Joe's eyes.

"I won't let the team down, Coach Joe. Thank you, sir."

Jeff looked up at Coach Joe and they shook hands and Jeff left the office and ran down the hallway with his game jersey.

Donna Wilson had a dilemma, of course. Should she purchase a Number 66 jersey with her brother's name on the back, or should she buy Tim's Number 11? Since the jerseys were sold with either the home blue and gold or the away white with blue and gold trim, Donna bought both. She worshipped her twin brother. He was a dink sometimes, but no one knew about Bobby's own personal scars except Donna, and of course, her mom.

Gwen Wilson bought her own Number 66. The bond between her and her children was deep and full. In its painful way, the searing burden borne by the Wilsons was a blessing. They loved each other in a way few families could understand. The welts on their arms, backs, and legs were the private places for their wounds.

Donna had her family, and soccer, and hockey. That was enough. Until Tim. She didn't plan on it. She was fine with just being friends. She saw the line Tim had to walk being a good athlete and also the son of a famous coach. She saw how he struggled with the difficulties of respecting Coach Joe's rules and the unwritten codes of just being in high school, with the drinking, and the drugs, and the temptations, and the pressures of living up to some impossible expectation that never came from his dad, but only came from someplace deep inside Tim. Donna wore Tim's game shirt when she went to bed, and he was the first thing she thought about when she woke up each morning.

Chapter 21

More Than a Game

The state championship game played at Boston University Nickerson field ended up being a barn burner. Salem got off to a quick start with two long runs by Mike Sancouci. Beaumont came back and scored on a Staber short run, a long pass and catch from Zeke Jones to Bill Bradner, another bomb of a pass to Alex Jones, and two thunderous touchdowns from Quick Lou Zarro. Just like that, Beaumont was up 35-14 at half time. Coach Joe's half time speech was characteristically short.

"Keep it up. Keep giving it your best. Don't let Salem back in the game."

But that's just what happened. Jim Ryan caught fire. He ran in for a score after he intercepted a pass from Zeke. He hit Sancouci for two quick touchdown passes. And then, on a 3rd and long from his own 35-yard line, Quick Lou barreled in for a sure sack. Somehow, Ryan managed to duck under Quick Lou. Ryan tucked the ball away and faked out Alex Jones and raced down the sideline. He had one man to beat.

Tim turned on the jets and caught Ryan from behind. He slammed him into the turf. The ball flew from Ryan and was recovered by Bobby. Salem players yanked at the ball and punched Bobby in the groin and raked at his eyes. Bobby twisted away and jumped up with the ball in his hands. The Beaumont side of the stadium exploded and the steel girders under their feet bounced up and down. Donna Wilson screamed for her brother and for Tim and grabbed her friends and they almost fell out of the stands. It was the turning point in the game. The score was 35-35 with just under two minutes to go.

Now the Jones boys took over. Zeke took the snap and raced to his right for a quick first down. The clock stopped with a minute and a half to go in the game.

Beaumont had the ball on their own 40-yard line. Zeke lofted a pass to a streaking Bill Bradner down to the Salem 30-yard line. He was driven out of bounds by a swarm of Salem defenders. The clocked stopped with 55 seconds to go. Both sides of the stadium rocked in a frenzy.

Zeke hit Alex with a pass. The Salem players held Zeke down so time would run off the clock, but he shoved them off and jumped up and screamed for timeout. 42 seconds remained on the clock, first and ten, Beaumont ball on the Salem 30.

The Warriors jogged to Coach Joe. The Salem Witches looked gassed when they got to their coach on the sideline. The Warriors huddled with Coach Joe. He gave them three plays to run, all designed to get out of bounds and stop the clock. The Warriors broke from Coach Joe and immediately set up on the line of scrimmage. Zeke took the shotgun snap from center. He pumped deep to a streaking Alex and drew the Salem defenders out of position. He then rifled a pass to Steve Staber. Just as Steve was about to make the catch and race upfield along the sideline, Jim Ryan appeared. He dove and extended his finger tips and knocked the ball down. Second and 10 from the Salem 30-yard line, 33 seconds left. Clock stopped. The Salem fans screamed for their team to hold on. The next play, Zeke rolled to his left and raced for the sideline, but Sancouci drove him out of bounds. 3rd and 10, the ball still on the Salem 30, 25 seconds to go. It was the Beaumont team who looked gassed now. Zeke pulled them into the huddle.

"All right. I know you're tired. So am I, but we're not losing today. So suck it up. Let's go. Quick Lou, this one's for you. Gun right, motion left, 60 pass fly, fullback draw."

The shotgun snap zipped back to Zeke. He stood tall, the football held near his right ear like he was going to pass. Just before a blitzing Salem player crashed into Zeke, he brought the ball down and handed it off to Lou. Zeke crumbled under the collision. Everyone on the Salem side of the field thought this was a pass. It was not. Lou sidestepped one Salem defender and raced straight down the middle of the field. He stiff armed another Witch and shifted into his top gear. The goal line was in sight.

Sancouci and Ryan recovered just in time to see Lou race for the goal line. They hit him full force at the five-yard line. Other Salem players piled on to make sure Quick Lou stayed down. The officials scrambled to pull everyone off of the pig pile. They found Quick Lou at the bottom of the pile. He was in agony. He held the ball in one arm, but the other arm was bent in a sickening angle. The head referee called an official timeout and the medical staff raced to on to the field.

"I broke my arm!"

A hush fell on both sides of the stadium. Lou writhed in agony. The game doctor calmed Lou down as best he could.

"Let me get this splint on so we can get you to the sideline and into an ambulance."

The trainers from both teams helped Lou to the Beaumont sideline. Both sides of the stadium stood and gave Quick Lou a standing ovation. Coach Joe met Lou at the ambulance. He put his hand on Lou's forehead and wiped away some of the sweat.

"Get 'em, Coach. Win this!"

His parents went with Lou in the ambulance and they left the stadium and made their way down the boulevard on their way to Mass General Hospital. The fate of the Warriors was no longer in the hands of Quick Lou Zarro.

The mix of excitement and fear pulsed through both sides of the stadium. Students from Beaumont and Salem ran down the stands, ready to rush out to their victorious team.

Lou's run was amazing, but it used up precious clock time. It was first and goal on the Salem four-yard line and there were five seconds to go and Beaumont's best player was on his way to the hospital. Coach Joe looked down his sideline.

"Andy Jones. You're in for Lou."

Andy and Jeff Tony and Tim watched from the sideline. They saw the pig-pile and heard Lou's screams. But it didn't register exactly what that meant.

"Get in there! What are you waiting for?" Tim smacked Andy on the back of his helmet. Andy raced in and buckled his chin strap along the way.

Now all three Jones boys were in the game. It probably happened earlier in the season. But this was completely different.

"Right here! Right now!" Steve yelled inside the huddle. The rest of the team held hands and Zeke calmed them down.

"Ok, here we go. Alex, you take Bill's spot at slot back. Bill, go to split end. Drive hard to the middle of the field and get in the way of Ryan. Alex, you know what to do. Catch the damn ball and get in the end zone. Andy. You have to make the block on the left end. It's now or never boys. Ready, break!"

Beaumont raced to the line of scrimmage. At first, Salem didn't notice that Alex and Bill switched positions. But just before the ball was snapped, Sancouci saw the switch. He raced over to Alex's side of the field. The ball was snapped and Sancouci exploded over the line of scrimmage. Andy adjusted and flew into the charging Salem star. The two collided. Sancouci knocked Andy backward, but the effort proved fatal to Salem. Zeke jumped around Sancouci and raced toward the touchdown pylon. Bill ran his route perfectly and slowed up Jim Ryan just enough to allow Alex to get away. Zeke squared his shoulders and zipped the ball to his streaking brother. Alex adjusted his route slightly, extended his hands well away from his shoulder pads and pulled in the pass. He twisted his body and dove for the end zone. He took the football and reached out both hands and knocked the red pylon flying. The official raised his arms high above his head.

The Beaumont fans went seismically insane. Bobby's mom had to be held from falling off the end of a bleacher. The Staber family grabbed each other in delirium. Bill Bradner's father whooped and he ran up and down the track that surrounded the field. Daniel Russell's mom cried, and Jeff Tony's dad grabbed her and kissed her. Long.

And Quick Lou? He found out about the win when he and his parents entered the emergency room at Mass General. There was a TV on and a security guard watched the game and jumped up and down when Alex dove into the end zone and the Zarros joined the security guard and they yelled and they screamed and the hospital staff had to call extra orderlies and nurses and even some doctors to try to quiet the disturbance.

In spite of the best efforts of the Boston City Police, Ike and Donna and the Beaumont student section and the team band stormed the field. Ike and Donna and the cheerleaders and the band and the Beaumont cops and the team managers and the team trainers and the school janitors and even the bus drivers crashed like a wave into the victorious Warriors. Ike tackled Bobby and knocked his friend off his feet. The crowd mauled them with hugs and screeches. Donna pushed through the crowd and found Tim and Andy at the back of the end zone. She leapt and the three crashed to the ground. Donna grabbed Tim and kissed him hard and Andy pulled them apart. He put both his hands on the side of Tim's face.

"I told you we would be champions together. Champions forever!"

And the three danced and more fans rushed onto the field and soon they were swamped under by the cheering and the crying and everything else that can only be felt when a high school wins a state championship.

Coach Joe? He took off his Beaumont hat and stood back and watched it all.

"My sons," was all anyone could make out and he said it again, and again, and again. "My sons."

Chapter 22

Smoke and Fire

The post-game party was epic. Former Beaumont players who were not able to make it to the game drove for hours to be part of the festivities. Even some parents came. They swallowed the embarrassment of being at a party with their kids, just to be part of a night that no one would ever forget.

Donna and Tim found it hard to be alone. It was impossible anyway. There were simply too many people celebrating. The two mingled and sang and danced and everyone roared with joy.

When the party finally wound down, Donna found Tim and gave him a deep kiss.

"I'm sorry I have to go. My ride is leaving. I'll see you tomorrow. Don't get a big head. You only made one good tackle!"

She shoved Tim away and moved off with her friends. He looked at her as she walked away. She took long, swaying strides and the light from the party shimmered around her. He never saw anything so beautiful. But before she piled into the car with her friends, over the din of the music and the laughter and the singing, she called out to him.

"One more thing. I love you!"

Her friends tickled her mercilessly and they pulled her in to the back seat and the car drove off. Tim watched Donna turn around in the back seat to face him and she and smile and waved and gave him the finger.

Andy and Bobby decided to walk home. The night was frigid and neither of them wore anything more than t-shirts. Andy's shoulder hurt from the hit he took from Mike Sancouci and Bobby's ribs ached.

"I freaking sucked today." Bobby moped down the street and cars raced past and horns were honked. "I was damn awful."

"What the hell, Bobby? We won! We're state champs for Christ's sake." Andy elbowed his friend. "What the hell are you talking about? You made big plays when we needed them."

Bobby reached into his back pocket and pulled out a bottle of Jack Daniels. He opened the bottle and took a long swig. His body shook from the cold.

"I'm freezing."

The two walked down the street. They looked into the dark and saw a lone driveway. Set back at the end of the driveway, they could see the skeleton of a partially built house. The roof was built and the plywood frame was in place.

"Let's get the hell inside."

The two walked down the dirt driveway and around the unfinished house and found an open window. Bobby gave Andy a boost and Andy tumbled through. He landed with a thump and a laugh. Andy lowered both hands and Bobby grabbed on and he ran up the side of the plywood and Andy heaved him in. The two rolled into the empty room.

"Shut the hell up. Someone will hear us. Damn." Bobby pulled out the Jack Daniels and let Andy take a long drink. "It's too dark in here."

He reached into his other pocket and pulled out a lighter.

"Grab some of those two by fours. I'm freezing. Let's get a fire going."

The two gathered up some of the leftover wood and stacked it up. Some carpenters left some newspaper in the corner of the unfinished room. In short order, they built up a good fire. The two moved close to the flames and warmed their hands and feet. The heat from the flames warmed their bodies and the alcohol did what it was supposed to do and they began to relax. Andy could see Bobby's eyes in the glow of the fire.

"You got something on your mind, Bobby?"

Bobby sat and waited a few moments before he spoke.

"Andy, how did it feel winning the game today without your dad around?"

Andy sat quietly and put his hands in his pockets. Bobby waited for his friend.

"I think my dad would have liked it today. I think he would have been proud of Zeke and Alex. I think he would have been proud of me, too."

Andy drew a deep breath. Aside from Coach Joe and Tim, he never talked about losing his dad to a heart attack. Letting Bobby in wasn't easy.

"Yeah, I think he would have been proud."

His words hung in the darkness and the light from the fire cast fitful shadows against the walls.

"You miss him."

"Yeah. I do miss him. I sometimes forget what he looked like. I know it hurts my mom and Zeke and Alex. They don't talk much about it."

The fire blossomed. Andy put his hand on Bobby's shoulder.

"Bobby, what about your dad? Did he die or something?"

Andy could see Bobby's breath even in the dark. He saw Bobby take a second, a third, and then a final gulp of the whiskey and throw the bottle against the wall. It bounced and landed in the fire. The label burned. The fire didn't seem to do anything to the glass.

"To hell with my old man." Bobby lay back and put his hands behind his head. "I'm glad the bastard wasn't here. He doesn't even know I play football, or Donna plays soccer, or even where we live. I want it to stay that way. He's a prick."

Bobby crossed one foot over the other and put his hands behind his head and closed his eyes. Andy sat crisscross on the cold plywood floor and stared at his friend. He wanted to ask Bobby more about his dad, but he didn't push it.

The whiskey took full effect. Bobby and Andy slowly closed their eyes and warmed themselves, and for different reasons, never felt as tired as they did right then.

Chapter 23

Breath of Life

Steve Staber had a huge Chevy wagon. The night became very cold and the champions were exhausted and the party was winding down and they needed to get home.

"Get in, you bastahds." Steve had a thick Massachusetts's accent. "Get in the cah!" Bill Bradner, Ike, Daniel Russell, Jeff Tony, and Tim jammed themselves in. The front seat was left for Quick Lou. When he got home from the hospital, even though he had a cast on his arm, he demanded his parents drop him off at the party. He was woozy with pain killers, but his parents relented, and Quick Lou celebrated with the town.

"Quick Lou gets shotgun. You bastahds ok with that?" Steve laughed and helped Quick Lou into the front seat. He carefully buckled the seat belt for his friend.

"Just get in the car, will you!" yelled Bill. He and Quick Lou were best friends, but Bill showed no mercy. "Jeez. We've been lugging you around all night."

"And I love you too, Bill." Quick Lou leaned back in his seat. He pulled a pair of cheap sunglasses out of his coat pocket and put them on dramatically. "Steve. Hit it!"

Steve 's car rolled down the street and the guys continued to float from their big win.

"I can't believe my arm snapped. I'm lying there and I see my arm going this way and that way."

With his good hand, he made an exaggerated snake-like motion. He held his cast up for the others to see.

"Yeah, we heard you scream. The whole stadium did, you baby!" Bill had a hand on Quick Lou's shoulder. He rubbed the enormous muscles behind Quick Lou's neck. "I thought we had no chance when you went down. But Andy Jones stepped up." The carload of friends talked about key plays in the game and how tough Salem played and they talked about Sancouci and Ryan and how Salem just never gave up.

"Andy doesn't make that block and Zeke gets stuffed," Steve mused as his car rolled on. "Andy got crushed, but he slowed down Sancouci just enough. It was the play of the game, really." The carload of friends cheered again. They broke out in song and sang the Beaumont Warrior fight song:

Oh, Beaumont High, all people cheer with voices loud and clear.

We will fight with honor and uphold the pride of the blue and gold!

They laughed and cried and sang horribly and bothered animals in the woods and woke sleeping children.

A mile or so along, Ike noticed a glow coming from the woods. "What the hell is that?"

"Looks like a fire. Jesus!"

Steve 's car turned down the driveway that led through a stand of trees in the direction of the blaze. A half-built house was on fire. Smoke billowed from the windows.

Bobby woke to flames spreading up the walls of the room.

"I fell asleep. Andy? Jesus, Andy!"

Andy lay face down on the floor. Bobby could hear a low moan coming from Andy as the flames continued to spread.

"My God!"

Bobby squatted down and grabbed Andy's waist. He heaved Andy over his shoulders. Panic set in, and Bobby's eyes flashed from wall to wall. The smoke choked him and he searched for some escape from the inferno but couldn't see anything.

"God, someone help!"

Bobby screamed, and the heat and the smoke began to overtake him.

Steve slammed the breaks and everyone jumped out. Ike raced toward the front door. He grabbed the door knob and had to quickly let go. It was so hot, it burned his hands. He pulled back his hands and then turned his head slightly to the side.

"I hear someone. Damn it. Someone's screaming!"

Steve and Jeff tried to peer into a window in the front of the house, but the smoke blinded them. Bill, Tim, and Daniel raced around back. Smoke and flames billowed from a burnt-out gap in the plywood.

"God, someone help!" they heard someone scream.

"It's coming from here. Tim, Daniel. Boost me up."

The two lifted Bill up to the open window. The fire spread fast.

"I see someone. Bobby is that you? Jesus! This way! Run!" Bill saw Bobby carry a dark figure on his shoulders.

"Throw him out! Do it, Bobby! Do it now!" Bill yelled at the top of his voice.

Bobby staggered through the dark smoke toward the voice. The opening in the wall appeared and Bobby heaved Andy out and then jumped behind him. They both crashed into Bill. The three of them plummeted to the ground. They slammed headlong into Tim and Daniel who broke their fall. Steve , Jeff, and Ike came around the corner followed by Quick Lou. Ike had water bottles from Steve 's car and he tried to douse Bobby and Andy. Steam rose from their bodies.

"Don't worry about me. Help Andy! Oh, God, help him."

With his good arm, Quick Lou grabbed Andy and the three of them managed to drag him along the slick, freezing grass and away from the burning house. Just when they were far enough away, the innards of the house collapsed and an explosion of flame rocketed into the nighttime sky. Tim slid next to Andy and put his ear on Andy's chest. He looked up at the others.

"He's not breathing."

Bobby heard panic in Tim's voice. He jumped on top of Andy and drove his clenched fists down into his chest.

"You're not dying on me, you bastard. You can't die on me!" Bobby thrust his clenched hands deep into Andy's chest. He pushed so hard the rest of the friends thought he might break Andy's ribs.

"No, Andy. Please, Jesus. You're not dying! You're not dying!" Bobby sobbed and pumped and tried to bring his friend back.

His thrusts into Andy's chest weakened and slowed as he began to lose strength. Bobby coughed and tried to suck air into his lungs and Tim saw that Bobby had nothing left, so he pushed him off and jumped on Andy.

"I got this."

He thrust down once and again and again and finally, Andy coughed and gasped for air and rolled over on his side.

"What the hell?" He coughed and spat and tried to get air into his lungs. "What happened?"

He worked to get up on his knees with the help of his friends. Bobby pushed them away and grabbed Andy by his t-shirt.

"Don't you ever die on me again, you piece of crap. Never do it again!"

Bobby broke down and cried and pulled Andy close. Everyone grabbed on to Bobby and Andy and joined in the crying and they held on to each other and their sobs turned to laughter now that they saw their friend was alive.

They picked Andy up and carried him to Steve 's car. The friends heard sirens over the roar of the flames. They jumped in and slammed the doors shut. In the backseat, Bobby cradled Andy's head. Ike took some more water and gave it to Bobby and Andy to drink. Jeff and Bill took off their t-shirts and tried to rub some of the black from the fire away from Bobby and Andy's eyes. Jeff sat on his knees and massaged Bobby's shoulders. Quick Lou looked back from the front seat. He couldn't believe that no one died. The adrenaline from what just happened blocked the pain from his broken arm. Steve rammed his car in gear and they raced down the driveway and made a hard right onto the main road, just as two cop cars crested a hill and flew toward the flames. A fire truck chased after them. The cop cars sped past Steve 's car. Tim looked out the back window. The cops didn't seem to slow down and they took a turn at full speed toward the burning corpse of a house.

Word of the fire spread quickly through the town of Beaumont. The police questioned neighbors who lived nearby. Everyone said that there was a big party, but that was about it. It was late at night when the fire began so most of the neighbors had long since gone to bed. Many used ear-plugs to drown out the wailing rock music, so they didn't hear the roar of the flames.

In the newspapers the next day, almost all the coverage focused on Beaumont's amazing state championship victory. Buried deep in the paper was a brief article about the burning down of an unfinished house. People didn't pay much attention.

Chapter 24

Cold Rain

On Sunday, Tim met Donna at the downtown park not far from East Junior High. He carried hot chocolate and donuts. The two shared a kiss and held each other against the cold. They finished their hug with their foreheads touching lightly. Donna took a sip of the hot chocolate. It burned her tongue just a bit, so she held it in her hands and blew air across the little opening in the Styrofoam cup.

"Are you OK? Bobby came home early in the morning. Funny. He reeked of smoke. Not cigarette smoke. Like something burning smoke. As usual, Thor didn't talk. He kissed my mother and helped her to bed. He gave me a little shove as he went past me into his bedroom. He told me you did ok last night before he shut himself off in his room. That's the first time he ever gave you a compliment. He was talking about the game, right?"

"Of course," and Tim looked into her eyes. He knew Donna knew about the fire.

"Yeah. We were at the fire. Staber, Zarro, Ike, Jeff Tony, Daniel, Bill Bradner, Quick Lou."

"Andy and Bobby? They were there too?"

"Yes. They were there." Tim looked away.

"You guys had something to do with the fire."

Donna took her hands and turned his head to face her.

"Yes. Andy and Bobby were in the house. They set the place on fire, but I don't think they meant to. They almost died because they were stupid and the only reason Andy is still alive is because your brother brought Andy back from the dead. And they were both drunk. But you probably knew that. Your brother and Bobby set the place on fire. They were drinking after the party and they walked home and went into the house and started a fire to stay warm and the place lit up after they fell asleep. We were driving home when we saw the fire. It was just dumb luck that we drove home that way. We got them out, but I swear we thought they were going to burn to death. Andy wasn't breathing when we pulled him away from the fire. Your brother wouldn't let Andy die. He just kept pumping on Andy's chest, over and over. I think the rest of us would have given up on Andy, but your brother just kept pumping. I swear, I thought Andy was gone."

Tim hung his head and thought about Bobby and Andy and how they barely made it out and how Andy lay there blackened by smoke from the fire.

The two sat on the bench. The wind bit into Donna and she brought her knees up to her chest. She rested her chin on her knees and looked across the park. It was too cold for families to be out and the threat of rain was heavy. The thrill of the state championship was gone. She leaned close to Tim and felt a light drizzle begin to fall. Tim almost lost his best friend. Donna shivered at what might have happened to her brother.

"I'm not sure what to say. A thank you just doesn't seem enough. Bobby gone? It would have killed my mother. I mean, it would have, literally, killed her."

Donna looked at Tim.

"And you. I might have lost you, Tim. I've already lost enough. And I just found you."

She held him closer and their hearts beat together while cars drove pass the park and the people in them didn't notice and the rain came down harder.

Chapter 25

Moving Pictures

Coach Joe sat at the kitchen table. He ate his breakfast slowly. The newspaper was filled with long articles about yesterday's triumph. There were pictures of Alex's catch, Lou's run, Sancouci and Ryan, even one of Tim pulling down Ryan and Bobby's fumble recovery. The picture on the front of the sports page showed Zeke and Alex holding the championship trophy skyward surrounded by their teammates. This wasn't Coach Joe's first championship, but it might have been the best. Everything came together. And his son. Coach Joe allowed himself a moment of pride. That was his kid who perhaps saved the game with his tackle on Jim Ryan. The morning was just about perfect.

Coach Joe heard Donna's car in the driveway. The door closed and Tim walked up the steps of their front porch. His winter coat was soaked and his hair was matted down. He sat next to his dad.

"Sleep much last night, dad?"

"Not really. The other coaches and some friends came over. We had quite a night."

Tim noticed a recycling bag filled with leftover pizza and Chinese containers and lots of beer cans. Tim looked at his dad.

"I had a couple of beers myself."

Coach Joe smiled and Tim tousled his hair.

"I suppose you earned a couple beers."

Tim slid his hand down onto his dad's shoulder. His dad playfully swatted it away.

"I hope you had a good night, Tim." There was a gleam in Coach Joe's eye. "Did you see Donna?"

"When did you find out about Donna and me?"

"Son. Really? I know I'm a football coach. It doesn't mean I'm a dumb football coach."

"Ok, I saw Donna. I went to a party. The place was packed."

"And everyone had a good time?"

"Yes, dad. We had a good time."

Tim sat and looked at his dad for a moment.

"I don't drink, Coach. You know that."

"Yes, I know you don't."

Now it was Coach Joe's turn to tousle Tim's hair.

"You did well in the game, son."

"Thanks, Dad. It was a long day. I hurt everywhere. But I'm freezing right now. I have to take a hot shower."

Tim got up off his chair and ran up the stairs. His dad's eyes followed him. When he heard the shower go on, Coach Joe turned back to the newspaper to cut out some of the articles to put in a scrapbook he secretly kept for his son

There were pictures of Tim when he played football and basketball in junior high. He traced his fingers over a picture of Tim and Andy in different uniforms when they played against each other in Pop Warner ball. They must have been eleven or twelve. There was even a picture of Tim and the Jones boys not too long after their father died of a heart attack. He pulled out a picture stuck in a slot on the last page of the scrapbook. He held it up and looked at a picture of a much younger man and a pretty wife with light brown hair and a two-year old boy swinging from his parent's arms. He looked at the faded picture and rubbed some dust off of it and then gently put it back into the slot on the back page. He sat for a long time by himself in the kitchen and listened to the sound of his son in the shower and the soft noise of the turning of the felt pages.

Chapter 26

Scrubbed Away

Andy woke up in his bedroom. His clothes were stripped off and his body scrubbed. His room smelled of smoke as he struggled to get up. He coughed and hacked up some gobs of black mucous and he remembered it all. He remembered sneaking into the house. He remembered drinking too much of the Jack Daniels. He remembered starting a fire with Bobby to keep warm. He remembered wishing his dad had seen the game. He remembered waking up with Tim straddling his chest in the cold of the night. He remembered hardly being able to breathe and then being thrown in the back of Steve 's station wagon. He remembered his mother crying hysterically when Bobby and Tim and Steve carried him into the house and Zeke and Alex helped him to the shower and stripped him and ran cold water all over his body. He remembered his brothers in the shower with him with their soaked clothes. They scoured the soot off his body and toweled him off and picked him up and carried him to his room and placed him gently into his bed and took turns watching over him.

Andy lay back down on his bed and said a little prayer of thanks that his mother didn't have to bury someone else in her family.

After Andy was put to bed and Mary kissed her son, she came out of Andy's bedroom and rushed at Steve and Tim and the rage inside burst like a wooden damn holding back water from a flood.

"Tell me! You tell me the whole thing!"

Steve and Tim took turns and they told her everything about their ride home and the fire and finding Bobby and Andy.

"You know what this family has been though! You know what we've lost. I couldn't bear to lose him, too. Not my Andy."

She turned to face Tim. Her face was drawn tight and her eyes blazed.

"You and Andy have been best friends forever. You should have never let this happen!"

Tim bowed his head slightly. Mary reached down and lifted Tim's chin so his face was level with hers and she slapped him with her open palm. The shock of it spun Tim's neck around. He rocked backwards and put up both hands to try and deflect the next slap he knew was sure to come, but it never did, and he covered his face with his hands and he tried to keep it all in, but it burst out.

"I'm sorry. Mrs. Jones, my God, I'm so sorry."

Tim turned and ran out the door and Mary stood there and watched him run down the driveway and Steve followed and Zeke and Alex kept their mom from collapsing.

They put their arms around her and led her to the family couch and helped her sit down. Mary Jones took long, deep breaths and her sons waited until she was ready to talk. Finally, her words poured out.

"I can't believe I slapped Tim. Seeing Andy like I did almost broke me. I saw Andy covered in soot and his clothes singed and I think I must have gone crazy. I can't stop from seeing my hand slap Tim's face."

Mary took another deep breath. Zeke stood up and paced across the worn rug that covered their family room. Alex shifted on the couch.

"I know you boys don't want to talk about it, but almost losing Andy just brought it all bubbling up and I couldn't hold it in. And I slapped Tim. For God's sake, what's wrong with me that I would do that to him?"

"Nothing's wrong with you, mom." Alex leaned in closer and took his mother's hand. "You might be the strongest person I know. When dad passed, God, mom, we were right there and we saw him die right before our eyes. We were insane when we tried to get the nurses and doctors to help, but he was gone. And you've held us all together. You've held it together for so long and when you saw Andy tonight, I thought you could take it, like you've always been able to do. Everything became too much for you, and you slapped Tim. It was wrong, but you did it and to be honest, mom, I thought you would have lost it a long time ago. So don't be so hard on yourself."

Mary looked back at Alex.

"I still remember the wake. Your dad looked so nice in that dark suit he always wore to church. It was the same one he wore when we got married. I remember how Coach Joe spoke at the funeral and his words were so kind and so strong. When we left the cemetery, Coach Joe and Tim and so many people came to the house. Tim sat with Andy all night and stayed over and was there when Andy woke up the next day. He's been such a dear friend to all of us."

Zeke pushed his fingers through his hair and then sat down again.

"Mom. I love you and I love you so much because you've made us all strong. Losing dad has been so hard for us. If I keep my feelings to myself, it's because I know you are being strong for all of us. And I think maybe tonight has been good for us, in a way. Maybe the shock of what happened to Andy was what we needed to open up about dad."

Zeke put his arm around his mother and so did Alex and the three of them sat for a very long time as Andy slept safely in his room just down the hallway.

Chapter 27

Bloody Elbows

Bobby left as soon as Andy was taken into the shower. He got home and helped his mother to bed and brushed past Donna and told her Tim did well and she looked at him and didn't know what he was talking about. Bobby's clothes smelled of beer and vodka and smoke and burned wood. He looked at the blisters on his hands from the heat of the flames and he tucked them under his armpits and rolled on his side. His elbows were scraped and bloodied from when he threw Andy out the window and jumped out after him.

Bobby remembered smashing his father's face with these same elbows and how blood gushed out of his dad's nose and mouth and how the police pulled Bobby off his dad.

He pulled his elbows under his chest and buried his face in the mattress.

Chapter 28

The Good and the Great

The story of the fire was an interesting addition to the news of the week, but soon it was blocked out by the clamor in town to honor this latest chapter of Coach Joe's championships. Of course, there was the obligatory banquet, usually open only to family members of the team, but there was such an outcry by many townspeople, the principal, Bill Dixon, decided to open the festivities to the public. Soon, 4,000 tickets were sold. They rented out the performing arts auditorium, the only place big enough that could hold that many people. Plans were made, and the big night arrived.

The players and coaches sat around tables set up on the auditorium stage. A family-style dinner was served and enormous amounts of food were consumed, mostly by the players. The JV and freshman teams were invited and they ate their share. When the meal was consumed, the Warrior players stacked desserts on paper plates while Mr. Dixon called everyone to take their seats. It was time to honor the Warriors.

Gifts were presented to everyone. The cheerleaders received bouquets of yellow roses. Many of them pressed the roses deep into their diaries. The team gave the band commemorative push pins. They wore them with pride at every concert they gave. They gave the team doctor, Jarvis Zinnipolous, a blue and gold stethoscope. The old doctor sobbed unabashedly upon receiving it from the Jones boys.

Every bus driver received blue and gold driving gloves. The team managers received the best gift of all. Coach Joe gave each manager tickets to Bruins games at the Boston Garden.

The assistant coaches received silver watches with blue and gold insets with "Beaumont Warriors" engraved on the back.

After the assistant coaches made their speeches and handed out JV and freshman awards, it was time to honor the varsity team. Each team member was called up individually by Coach Joe. The sophomores came first. Coach Joe called up Bobby and Andy and Tim and Jeff Tony to receive their varsity letters.

Then the juniors were announced. Steve , Bill, Daniel, and Quick Lou received their varsity letters. Coach Joe announced that the four of them had been selected captains. They stood proudly on the stage in front of their team and the crowd. Daniel leaned on a crutch. He was scheduled for surgery in the next few weeks. He hoped this would be an end to his pain. Bill looked into the crowd and saw his dad crying. Steve was majestic in his blue blazer with gold striped tie.

And then there was Quick Lou. While the other three stood seriously in front of the crowd, Quick Lou, received his varsity letter and he danced around the stage. He hugged his teammates and the coaches and the team managers and Dr. Z, and finally the cheerleaders. He planted kisses on the cheeks of each one of them and the crowd roared.

Finally, it was the seniors' turn to be honored. Coach Joe left Zeke and Alex for the end. Few people truly understood the bond the Jones boys and Coach Joe had for each other. Coach Joe still had dinner with the Jones boys once a month. He just kept showing up, unannounced. He had an uncanny way of arriving for dinner on days Mrs. Jones was feeling down, or the boys had homework issues or trouble with girlfriends. He even helped guide Zeke and Alex when it came for them to decide what college they would attend.

Zeke and Alex made quick speeches. They razzed their teammates over funny events that happened during the season. The crowd laughed when the brothers handed out joke gifts. Alex gave Tim a stopwatch. Tim never lost a wind sprint. He gave Andy a Bobblehead football player with a cracked helmet. Zeke gave

Bobby one of those party favors you blow and confetti flies out. The team laughed and Bobby even managed to smile.

Coach Joe made his speech. The crowd hung on every word. He spoke of integrity, and honesty, and compassion. He told the team they were special because they overcame so much to win. He told them there would be a day when they would lose and that people would judge them, not how they handled winning, but how they handled losing. He looked at Zeke and Alex and Andy, and Coach Joe looked out in the audience and he saw Mary. She wiped a tear from her face with her tissue she kept in the sleeve of her dress.

Principal Dixon finished the banquet with gifts purchased by a fundraiser organized by the town. He called up each player and presented them with a wrapped box. He asked that the box remain sealed until he gave the order. The crowd gasped when each player held high their brand-new varsity letter jackets. Each jacket was blue with gold arm sleeves. A "B" was hand stitched over the heart of each jacket, and the team name "Warriors" was emblazoned in gold on the back. Zeke and Alex had big "C"s on their jacket. Their leadership had been true all season. The local seamstress in town made sure that Steve, Bill, Daniel, and Lou also had their captain's "C" sewn on their jackets, ready to be captains for the next year.

The banquet ended and the crowd streamed out. Families and close friends hung around and waited for the team to finally leave the stage area. Mrs. Wilson and Donna waited patiently for Bobby to join them. When he broke through the crowd, he hugged his sister. She beamed, but also gave him a knowing look. She was just happy her brother was still alive. Mrs. Wilson pulled Bobby close. She did not know how close she had been to losing her son.

Tim came and joined the Wilson family. He hugged Mrs. Wilson. Donna intertwined her fingers in Tim's hand. He then turned to Bobby.

"You had a fine season. All-Conference as a sophomore. You deserved it."

"Screw you," he said back to Tim with a smirk, but he also extended a hand.

The two shook and looked each other in the eye.

"Thanks, you dink."

Bobby held on to Tim's hand for a bit and he looked at him and his eyes softened. The "Thanks" Bobby shared with Tim went well beyond a handshake.

Gwen put her arms around her son and Bobby and Tim released their handshake. Bobby held his mother and sister, and friends swirled around and the coaches left the stage and the season ended.

Chapter 29

Repeat

It looked to be a sensational junior year for Tim, Andy, Bobby, and the much-improved Jeff Tony. Jeff sprouted an extra four inches over the summer and put on about 25 pounds. He now stood 6'3, and weighed 210 pounds. Daniel Russell started the season as first-string quarterback, but it was a difficult decision for Coach Joe. There was little difference between Daniel and Jeff. But Daniel got the nod to start, and Coach Joe decided to start at Jeff at split end, taking over for the now graduated Alex Jones. Daniel and Jeff made a fabulous quarterback, receiver tandem. It seemed that every pass Daniel threw to Jeff, he somehow made the catch.

The backfield of Quick Lou Zarro, Bill Bradner, and Steve Staber returned after their fabulous junior year and state championship. So once again, Tim and Andy were on the outside looking in. But to Coach Joe, the two friends were too good not to play. Andy was now the principal backup to all three running backs. And he would also start at one of the outside linebackers with "Wild Man" Bobby Wilson.

Tim returned as the starting free safety, with Daniel focusing just on quarterback. Coach Joe also inserted Tim as the other starting split end, opposite Jeff Tony. In some respects, Coach Joe looked at his offensive starters and recognized that losing the older Jones brothers was not going to be an issue. The preseason polls had the Beaumont Warriors as the clear favorite to repeat as state champions.

Meanwhile, Donna turned into the best soccer player in the state. College coaches from all of the country came to her games. On some days, the sideline was packed with coaches from Notre Dame or Texas or UCLA or ever the reigning national champion University of North Carolina Tar Heels. She was, simply, impressive. She made bicycle kicks for goals and outran everyone. She was tough and could not be intimidated by players from other teams. During one game, a kid from Methuen got in a fight with one of Donna's teammates. Donna raced across the field and grabbed the Methuen's kid's fist. Donna held the fist and glared at the Methuen kid and she backed down and that ended the fight. It was the same day as the North Carolina coach stood on the sideline. He made some notes on a yellow pad of paper and nodded his head a few times.

Donna trained all summer with Tim and Jeff. She lifted weights with them. She ran stairs with them. She even ran pass patterns with them. She was as fast as Jeff. Donna pushed her friends mercilessly.

"You guys work hard. Even you, Tim."

She laughed and stood over them with her hands on her hips while Tim and Jeff lay on the ground and moaned and tried to catch their breath. She squatted down next to Tim and Jeff and she reached over and punched Tim in the gut. She laughed at him when he rolled over into a ball. Jeff jumped in and elbowed Tim in the back, and a fake fight erupted between the three friends. Finally, Donna stood up and put one foot on Tim's back and the other on Jeff's. She howled like a coyote and put both of her arms high into the air in triumph. She dropped back down and lay next to Tim. Their bodies glistened with sweat and she reached over and held his hand. Jeff sat nearby in a spread eagle and grinned at the pair.

"You want I should leave you two alone?"

Donna and Tim grinned at each other and jumped up and pounced on Jeff, burying him in laughter and fake punches.

"Get off me, you freaks!"

The three untangled and lay on their backs and squinted up into the hot, Massachusetts late afternoon sky, and everything was good.

Chapter 30

Broken Promises

The Beaumont Warriors football team got off to a great start. They were 5-0 entering a pivotal game with their rivals, Methuen. Late in the first half, Daniel dropped back to pass and lofted a perfect spiral to Tim who cradled the ball and raced untouched 60 yards for a touchdown. Both of them were having electric years. Some colleges began to come to watch Daniel and Tim.

As Tim tossed the ball back to the official, he saw Daniel slumped over in the middle of the field. He tried to put weight on his leg, but it buckled and teammates had to help Daniel to the sideline. The trainers met Daniel by the bench and put ice on his ankle. Coach Joe walked over.

"I'm sorry, son. Ankle again?"

"Yes, coach. Jesus, not again!"

Daniel ripped off his helmet and threw it aside. Coach Joe put a hand on Daniel's shoulder pads. The trainer taped some ice to Daniel's ankle. Coach Joe left Daniel and walked back to the rest of the team. He spoke to Jeff and Ike.

"Jeff, take over at quarterback. Ike, take his spot at split end." Coach Joe made the change and the two players joined the huddle when Beaumont got the ball back on offense.

"Take us in, Jeff."

Steve signaled for the entire huddle to take hands.

"Got it. 38 toss, fake reverse left. Ready, break."

The Warriors raced to the line. The play was designed to make it look like Tim was going to take a reverse pitch from Steve. It worked earlier in the game. But this time, Steve would take the toss sweep to the right and fake a handoff to Tim. The idea was the defense would remember the play and take off after Tim. It worked brilliantly. Tim faked receiving the toss and raced in the opposite direction toward the left side of the field. The defense saw the play develop and crashed across the line of scrimmage and drove Tim into the turf. The fake was so well done, the officials thought, for a brief moment, that Tim still had the ball. He didn't. Steve raced down the Beaumont sideline unnoticed until it was too late for the Methuen defenders. When Steve crossed the goal line, Bill Bradner and Quick Lou jumped on Steve's back and the three tumbled to the ground. 28-7, Beaumont, as time expired for the first half. One play with Jeff Tony at quarterback and the Warriors scored. Not a bad start.

The second half began with a long run by Methuen for a touchdown. This fired up the Warriors. When they got the ball back, Coach Joe unleashed the strong arm and quick feet of his new quarterback. Jeff threw a dart to Bill Bradner for 20 yards. He hit Ike on a quick curl pass over the middle for another 10 yards. He scrambled out of the pocket and eluded two Methuen defenders and escaped down the sideline. Tim broke off his pass route and threw a crushing block that knocked the chasing Methuen defender right into the Methuen bench. Jeff ran the remaining fifteen yards to the end zone. 35-7, Beaumont.

Jeff ended the game 17-20, 255 yards passing with two touchdown passes, one to Ike and one to Tim. He also scored on a zig-zag run of his own. Final score, Beaumont 49, Methuen 14.

The team got on their bus and headed home. Bobby sat in the back and made room for Daniel. Daniel's ankle was swollen and the ice packs drooped. He put his bad ankle up on the seat next to Ike.

"I don't give a rat's ass that Jeff had a good game. I'm not losing my starting job just because I got hurt. Coach Joe can't do that to me."

"Who says Coach Joe's taking your job away?" Ike put his hand on Daniel's shoulder. "You've played great all season. He wouldn't do that to you."

"Won't he? Coach Joe wants to win. Period. You watch what happens if we win a few games with Jeff at quarterback and me with my bad ankle. He'll keep me out."

Steve Staber overheard the conversation. He turned around in his seat. He spoke in his strong voice.

"Don't give him a reason to keep you out. Bust your ass. Yeah, Coach Joe wants to win. We all do. You earned your spot at quarterback this season, but that doesn't mean you own the starting job. You got hurt. What was Jeff supposed to do, go out and stink? He played his best and it worked out today. That doesn't mean he owns the job any more than you do. When you get healthy, practice hard. Coach Joe will see it."

"Yeah, Steve, it's easy for you to say that. No one has challenged your starting running back spot."

"I get hurt and Andy takes my place. Or he moves Tim to running back. Then I fight my way back into the starting line-up. That's how it works."

"I've been hurt so many times, I bet Coach Joe's been looking for a shot to replace me."

"You're wrong, Daniel. Jesus."

"You better be right, Steve."

Daniel eyed Steve and then bent over and adjusted the ice packs. They dripped all over the floor of the bus. Bobby put his arm around Daniel.

"Don't worry, Daniel. You're the best quarterback we've got. Right Andy and Ike?"

They both nodded and looked across at Steve and everyone looked at each other suspiciously and they all hoped everything they said was true. Tim sat a few seats away and heard it all and wondered the same thing.

Chapter 31

My Job

Daniel planned a party that night for after the game. Beaumont's win streak had ballooned to 36 games. It was a reason to celebrate. Tim told Coach Joe he was going out to the movies with Donna, but they changed their minds and ended up at Daniel's house. There was a wild party going on when Donna parked her car across the street from Daniel's house. She and Tim got out of the car and held hands and walked around behind Daniel's house and entered the basement door. Donna walked in first. Tim hesitated and then followed in after her. Donna waited for Tim and saw the look on his face change. His smile left him and his brow furrowed.

"You hate this." Donna handed him some water. People smoked and drank and danced. "But you still come to these parties. Why?"

"I hate this." He gestured at some kids smoking and drinking. "But I like them." He nodded to the clumps of kids who came in to the party or left to do something else.

"Why don't you ever have people over? I mean, I'd swing by, I suppose."

She planted a quick kiss and pulled him close. As she held him, Andy, Bobby, and Daniel stumbled out of a back room. They each had a beer in their hands and a cloud of smoke hung over their heads. Donna stepped toward her brother.

"You had enough yet, Bobby?"

"There's never enough. Not with these two." He grabbed Andy and Daniel around the neck and yanked them close. "Best damn players on the team!"

"Hell, yeah. The best players on the team."

Andy swayed and Bobby caught him.

"And Daniel Russell is the best quarterback this town has ever seen." Bobby thrust another beer at Daniel. "The best, evah!" Bobby yelled and Daniel put the beer to his mouth and guzzled it down.

"Yeah, the best evah."

Daniel staggered away to his left pass Bobby and Andy and he bent over and put his hands on his knees and threw up. Some of it spattered onto Tim's sneakers. Donna jumped back.

"God, Daniel. Watch out!"

Donna pulled Tim back and Daniel's stomach heaved again. Bobby and Andy roared with laughter.

"He's had quite a night. Isn't that right, Daniel?" Andy tried to help his friend wipe off the rest of the puke from his game jersey that he still wore from the game that afternoon.

"Coach Joe better not find out. Right Tim?" Bobby was close enough that Tim could not miss the stink of beer and the reek of dope. "What do you think, Tim? Gonna tell your dad we're stoned?"

Bobby put his hand on Tim's shoulder. Tim slapped it off.

"Freaking Coach Joe."

Daniel puked again, this time toward Jeff Tony who arrived with Quick Lou, Bill Bradner, and Steve Staber. The four newcomers jumped back. They looked at Daniel with amusement, but their grins didn't last long when Daniel fell to his knees and landed in a puddle of his own vomit. He coughed and spat out the last of the bile lodged in his throat. He tried to pull himself to his feet, but he slipped and sprawled on the basement floor. Bobby and Andy tried to help him up. Daniel shoved them away.

"It's my job. It's mine when I get back, Jeff."

He finally got up and shook off Bobby and Andy. Daniel grabbed Jeff by the collar and pulled him close. Jeff tried to push Daniel away and once again, Daniel slipped and landed on his backside. He was covered with puke and beer.

"You're drunk, Daniel."

Jeff's face was red. Bobby stepped toward Jeff and twisted him around and shouted in his face.

"Enjoy your time at quarterback, Jeff! It ain't gonna last."

Bobby belched and smiled at Jeff, but there was no warmth to it.

"Daniel is our guy. Ain't that right, Andy?" Bobby whacked Andy on the back. "Daniel should start at quarterback this Friday."

Andy felt the walls of Daniel's basement close in. Bobby took another swig of beer. Andy looked at Tim and then Daniel. It took Andy too long to answer and there wasn't much conviction in his voice. It came out in a low sound like he was trying to pull it back it.

"Daniel's been our quarterback all year. When he gets healthy again, he should have the job."

Andy looked at Tim who held his stare. Andy's eyes darted away and he took a step back behind Bobby.

"Hell, yeah."

Bobby put an arm around Andy and pulled him back around so he stood in front. Jeff finally stepped forward. He had enough of what Bobby had to say, and Andy. He stood almost nose to nose with Bobby.

"Hey, you got hurt, Daniel, and Coach Joe put me in. What was I supposed to do?"

Bill, Steve , and Quick Lou moved to Jeff's side. So did Tim, and then Donna. Ike showed up and gave some paper towels to Daniel. He walked over and stood behind Bobby and Andy.

Daniel tried to wipe the crap off his game shirt, but instead managed to smear the puke stain into his number 12. The team was split in two. Donna faced Bobby and Andy.

"You guys won today. So why fight about who might play quarterback and what Coach Joe might do? What is it, like 35 straight games you've won in a row?"

"36!" Everyone corrected her, even Daniel, who seemed to sober up.

"36 games in a row? Big deal. Getting stoned and drunk is going to keep your win streak alive? Do you guys really believe that? You think you can keep partying and you'll keep winning and you'll keep partying and around and around she goes and nothing will knock your happy train off the track? You're stupid if you think you're immortal. The fire last year should have taught you that. You're lucky no one died!"

Spit flew from Donna's mouth and everyone stepped back from her. Even Tim looked startled.

"I've had enough of the bullshit and the parties and the pressures you guys put on each other game after game, like if you don't win another state championship the town will fall apart. It makes no sense to me, but what the hell do I know? You guys are kings and everything you do makes you worthy of worship. It's bullshit." No one moved or spoke or even breathed. Donna walked over to her brother and grabbed him by the arm and yanked him toward her car. Tim expected Bobby to struggle, but surprisingly, he let himself be pulled away from the party by his sister. She opened the front door for him and Bobby fell in and Donna yelled at him to put on his seat belt and he did and she started the car and rolled down her window.

"The party's over. Go home, all of you, before you make bigger fools out of yourself. It's just football!"

She hit the gas and the car lurched out of Daniel's driveway. The party broke up and kids spilled beer out of their bottles and finished their joints if they were smoking them and shuffled off toward their own cars, basically because Donna just told them to do so. Daniel shook his head and slipped once more on his puke. He grabbed Jeff by the sleeve of his hoodie and the two stared at each other for a bit. Daniel let go and walked through his dark basement and climbed the stairs to his dark house. Tim and Steve and Bill and Bobby and Lou and Ike and Jeff watched Daniel climb the basement stairs and shut the door behind him and they turned around and left the party without saying anything to each other.

Chapter 32

Bad Dreams

Tim got home early. Coach Joe sat in a chair and went over game stats and the injury report.

"That didn't last long. You and Donna have a good time?" He spoke to Tim without looking up. "You two ok?"

"Come on, dad."

Tim took a deep breath.

"Did you go to the movies or something?"

Coach Joe looked up from his work.

"We were going to go, but we ended up at Daniel's house with the rest of the guys."

Tim got a drink of water from the faucet.

"How's Daniel's ankle? He has to be frustrated. He's played well this year."

Coach Joe looked back down at the stats.

"His ankle's better, I think."

Tim finished his water and held the glass in his hand.

"How's Andy? I don't see the two of you together much. Except at games. Was he there tonight?"

"He was there. With Bobby."

Tim put down the glass.

"Bobby has become good friends with the both of you. That's good. Three good leaders."

"You think so?"

He made a grunt and took the glass and rinsed it out and put it back in the cabinet. Tim remembered how his friends had split into two groups about who should play quarterback. Tim had stood beside Jeff. Lines on the team were now drawn, and Tim clearly was on one side. Coach Joe took a deep breath and yawned.

"Well, get some sleep."

Tim turned and walked upstairs and felt like he was going to be sick. He lay down on his bed and felt like a Civil War general. He could see the battle about to take shape. Tim imagined sending troops in a charge, knowing that he had to follow orders and they would all be killed and there was nothing he could do to stop it. He saw the slaughter in his mind again and again, his troops being cut down by an enemy that was shadowed in the fog of war. Finally, he fell asleep with the image of being overwhelmed by the carnage of a battle while a single bayonet pierced his heart.

The Beaumont Warriors continued to roll. Jeff Tony made the quarterback position his own. Against Lowell, he set a league record 548 yards passing and six touchdowns. Tim set his own record, hauling in five of those touchdown passes. Ike caught the other. Quick Lou, Steve, and Bill each rushed for scores as the Warriors routed Lowell 63-21. Bobby and Andy dominated on defense. Bobby had three sacks and Andy had a fumble recovery and an interception to go along with eight tackles. The two friends had become the best linebacking crew in the state, along with Steve Staber. Daniel Russell watched from the sidelines. His ankle felt better. He watched Jeff Tony make one great pass after another. Tim watched Daniel from the sidelines and it was like he could see smoke coming out of Daniel's ears.

Chapter 33

Carolina

Donna had quite a week or her own. She scored four goals against Lowell. This put her one goal away from the state record for most goals scored in a season. There were articles about her in the local papers and requests for interviews which she declined. But the state knew about Donna Wilson because she was simply the best soccer player in the state.

That night, she took a phone call.

"Yes, sir. Yes. Thank you. Thank you very much, coach."

She hung up the phone. Her mom and Bobby ate cold meatloaf sandwiches and instant mashed potatoes. They turned to face Donna.

"What is it?" Donna's mom stood up from the table. "Tell me, dear."

"Sorry mom, I gotta go."

Donna rushed pass her mom and grabbed her Beaumont soccer sweatshirt and her car keys. She swung open the kitchen door and ran to her car and gunned it and flew out of the driveway. Bobby turned back to his meatloaf.

"Probably going to Tim the Prick's."

He stuffed meat into his mouth with a grunt. Donna's mom sat back down next to her son.

"Did you get a chance to see Donna play the other day?" Gwen looked at her son.

"Saw the end of the game after my practice. Saw her knock a header over the Lowell goalie." A slight grin formed on his face. "She's really good." He went back to eat more meatloaf.

Gwen stood up and walked to the sink and took her plate and washed it and put it back on the drying rack.

"I still worry about you two." Gwen wiped her hands on her apron and sat back down. Bobby stopped eating.

"I know you do." He got up and scraped off some potatoes from his plate and it fell with a thud into the trash can. "But she's ok." Gwen put her hand on Bobby's.

"And what about you? We don't talk much anymore."

She looked at her son.

"I'm fine. School's good. I'm playing well. That's it."

He washed off the rest of his plate. He took a sponge and wiped off the kitchen table and then the sink. He cleaned out the sponge and placed it back against the edge of the counter top.

"It's been a few years since we left Ohio, Bobby. We've never talked about what happened. Maybe it's time we did."

Bobby turned away from his mother and stared outside the kitchen window. He reached over and picked up a wet towel from the counter. He balled it up and turned quickly and reared back and threw the wet towel against the wall by the refrigerator. The moisture from the towel made it stick for a moment before it slid down onto the floor.

"Christ, mom. I don't want to talk!"

"You're still so angry. Please, Bobby."

She tried to put her arms around him, but he shrugged her off and stormed out of the kitchen and ripped open the door to his bedroom and slammed it shut. Gwen stood in the kitchen and heard the boom of the door. She sat back down at her chair and put her head in her hands and she tried to control her breathing which she couldn't seem to do and music blared from Bobby's bedroom. She sat for a while, and when she stopped crying and got her breathing under control, she stood up and wiped ketchup and a few chunks of meatloaf off her work clothes. She walked to her own room and lay on her bed and thought about the night Bobby saved her from being beaten to death and she knew no boy should have to save his own mother from the hands of a monster, even if the monster was Bobby and Donna's dad.

Donna's car spun into Tim's driveway. The wheels on her car screeched when she hit the brakes. She leapt out of the car and ran up the front stairs. Tim and Coach Joe ate frozen lasagna. She raced in without knocking and grabbed Tim's hand and pulled him from the table.

"Hello, Coach Joe! I need your son."

"Hello to you, too."

Coach Joe sat at the kitchen table. He held a fork full of lasagna suspended near his mouth.

Donna pulled Tim out of the kitchen and through the front door and around to the side of his house and pushed him down on the grass.

"What the hell? Dad and I were just about to eat some high-quality frozen lasagna."

"Carolina!"

"What about Carolina?"

"They offered. Carolina offered me a full scholarship!"

"Don't shit me. Don't you shit me, Donna Wilson!"

She rolled Tim over and got on top of him.

"Carolina? You got offered a scholarship from Carolina?"

Donna pinned Tim's hands above his head.

"Yes, you idiot. Carolina. Carolina offered me a scholarship. Full ride!"

She pressed down against him and kissed him hard. She rolled him over a few times until they were hidden behind a large oak tree and they fumbled with their clothes in the heat of the day.

Afterwards, when it was dark and most of their clothes were back on and their breathing was finally under control, they looked up into the night time sky. A single dot of light moved in the stars. A satellite made its singular journey.

"I'm so happy."

Tim let out a long sigh.

"I know you're happy. But what about my scholarship?"

"Yeah, I'm happy about that too."

The two laughed. Donna twirled some of Tim's hair as her head lay upon his chest.

"Donna Wilson is going to be a North Carolina Tar Heel. You know, they have a pretty good team."

"Uh, yeah. Like, national champion good!" She looked up at him as he held a smirk. "Wait, did you just get me?"

"Well, you do it to me all the time. I thought I would do the teasing at least once."

He let his smirk turn into a wide smile and he pulled her to his face and kissed her again."

"I guess I deserved that."

"Yes, you did deserve that. And the scholarship too."

The two of them burst out a laugh and the faintest light of dawn slowly dimmed the stars.

Chapter 34

Dented Metal

Each Wednesday, Coach Joe listed the depth chart. Nothing changed from last week, except Daniel Russell's name was back on the chart. When he saw it, he spun away and shoved pass some of his friends. Practice was about to begin.

The first team defense took the field. The second-string offense wore yellow scrimmage vests and red skull caps. Coach Joe's rules were that everything was full speed except for the tackling. That was to be done in "thud" form: eyes up, flat back, wide base, wrap up, drive the legs. And that was it. No full tackling and never drive a man into the ground. Coach Joe wanted to keep his team healthy.

The second string huddled.

"What the hell does he want us to run?"

Daniel scowled out of the huddle and Coach Joe sent in a play.

"Gun, trips right, 62 pass all fly."

The second stringer shared the play with Daniel. Daniel called out the play and half-heartedly broke the huddle. The team ran to their positions, but Daniel just walked to his. He stood with hands on his hips and spat out of his facemask. A drip of it hung on the plastic.

"Set, hut."

The ball was snapped and Daniel caught it and walked back three steps. He looked down field and saw all four of his receivers running deep. He stepped to his right and almost no effort, he tossed the ball listlessly down field. It landed 20 yards short of the nearest receiver.

Tim saw Daniel make the throw. He knew Daniel could throw a ball 50 yards, even with a bum ankle. It pissed Tim off. It pissed off Steve, Quick Lou, and Bill. Steve let Daniel know it.

"Come on, man. Make the throw!"

"Screw you," Daniel mumbled and he returned to the huddle. Coach Joe saw Daniel's lame pass and heard his mumble. He stepped back and folded his arms. The quarterback situation had to play itself out.

The practice dragged. Sometimes a team gets sucked into the negativity of one guy. This was one of those times. When practice was over, Coach Joe called everyone into the huddle.

"As you know, I have two big team rules. One is no partying. The other is, you give your teammates your best. Every practice and game. I don't expect these rules to be followed because I make them. I expect these rules to be followed so you can grow up. Show your teammates how you handle things when they aren't going well. That's the true measure of a man."

He slowly looked around at his team. His eyes settled on Daniel. They locked eyes until Daniel broke his stare and looked down at his football cleats.

"Captains, break them off."

Coach Joe moved away from the huddle and made his way toward the locker rooms. His assistant coaches joined him.

Daniel walked toward the locker rooms with Bobby and Andy.

"What the hell? You should be starting. That's crap!" Bobby cursed loudly and it reached the ears of Steve Staber, Tim, and Jeff Tony. Steve turned to face Daniel.

"Coach is doing what's best for the team. You know you'll get your shot again. Do your best."

Daniel poked Steve 's chest.

"Don't give me that horse crap rah, rah, bullshit, Steve. I started every game until I got hurt. We were undefeated. I should get my job back."

"Damn right, Steve." Bobby stepped toward the senior captain. Tim moved in between Bobby and Steve .

"Take it easy, the both of you. It will work out."

Tim kept a hand on the chest of both of his friends.

"And you stay the hell out of it." Bobby slapped Tim's hand away from his chest. "Daniel should be the starter. Andy, what do you think?"

Andy stood a few feet away. Another choice to be made.

"He was the starter before he got hurt."

Andy said it quietly, like he was being squeezed between two very large walls and no one could hear him. Daniel moved over next to Andy and Bobby and Ike joined them. Steve , Quick Lou, and Bill stood behind Tim.

"You want your job back? Well, today didn't help. You practiced like crap. You want to be our quarterback? Throw the damn ball." Steve barked at Daniel. "Earn your spot back. It's not owed to you. Work for it!"

"Screw you, too, Staber. You're supposed to look out for the seniors."

Daniel pushed his finger hard into Steve 's sternum.

"I'm supposed to look out for the team."

Steve grabbed Daniel's finger and twisted it.

"What the hell, Steve. Let go!"

Daniel yanked his hand away from Steve and grabbed his finger and bent over at his waist.

"Well, I better freaking start Friday night."

Daniel shoved Steve and walked off to the lockers with Bobby and Ike at his side. Andy trailed his three friends. He looked back quickly at Tim and saw his stare. He stopped for a moment and then put his head down and turned and followed Bobby and Daniel into the locker room and he slammed the door behind him.

"Well, I think that certainly turned out well."

The team laughed nervously at Quick Lou's joke. Tim grinned a bit, but he looked at the team as they shuffled toward the locker rooms and Tim felt a strain like a rope that had been cut with a knife and was about to snap.

Chapter 35

The Winning Streak

Donna picked Tim up at his house before the game. It was a ritual and the two didn't want to jinx the winning streak.

"You had a tough week."

She drove from Tim's house toward the high school. The Yellow buses stood end to end. The drivers ran the diesel engines and the exhaust cast a shadow over the locker room area.

"Yes."

"You got trouble, Tim"

"I know. Daniel thinks he should start."

"No, you got more trouble than just that. You sided with your dad. At least that's what Bobby thinks. Maybe Andy thinks so too. Things are ugly."

"Yes." Tim looked out the car window. It was a cold night and his breath began to fog up his side of the car. "And you've just made it clear that the team is split on this. A bunch of the guys think Daniel should start tonight, and a bunch think he hasn't earned his spot back. So yeah, you're right. It's ugly."

Donna looked at Tim and saw the crease in his forehead deepen and a vein in his neck bulge.

"Just play your best. Right now, that's all you got."

She leaned over and kissed him gently. Her right hand held his face. She dropped her forehead against his and the two sat quietly. After a moment, she leaned back.

"Get the hell out of my car. You have a game to play."

She smiled at him and shoved him teasingly toward the passenger door. Tim grabbed his backpack and stepped out. She drove off and his eyes followed. The sick feeling in his stomach returned and he turned and walked through the parking lot pass the belching buses and through the doors that led down to the lockers.

As usual, the team dressed quietly. Every man prepared himself in a different way. Quick Lou sat at his locker and listened to music. Ike paced back and forth and tried not to step on anyone's toes. Steve taped his wrists. Jeff Tony sat against his locker and looked off and made no eye contact with anyone. Everyone kept their distance from Bobby. A rumble came out whenever Bobby breathed in or out.

Tim put on eye black and taped his cleats and looked at Andy. Their eyes met for a moment and then Andy turned away. The locker room smelled of old towels and stinking socks and it was deeply hot in spite of the cold November night outside.

Tim sat up straight. The door from outside to the locker room area slammed open and Daniel strode down the hallway. He wore a jean jacket with the collar turned way up. The part of his neck that could be seen was beat red. Underneath his jacket, he wore a dirty t-shirt that could have been white at one time. His blue jeans were faded and stained and looked like they hadn't been washed in weeks. He had work boots that might have belonged to someone else a while ago. The laces were untied and they dragged behind Daniel as he walked down the hallway. He walked pass the lockers and looked in quickly but did not say anything to anyone. He stopped in front of the coach's office and twisted the door knob without knocking and walked inside and closed the door with a bit of a bang.

Tim watched Daniel walk into his dad's office. He felt vomit rising in his throat that he tried to keep down. Bobby stared at the office door. He didn't have to wait long before the damn burst.

"I should be starting and you know it, you mother fucker! I'm a senior and I'm better than Jeff Tony and the whole team knows it. They want me in! Start me, or I quit. I'll freaking quit."

The door swung open and Daniel stormed out.

"You made your choice then." Coach Joe's voice could barely be heard in the varsity locker area.

Daniel grabbed the knob and swung the door hard and the boom of it shook the lockers. He ran down the hallway and threw a punch against a gym locker. His fist dented the wire mesh. He flew out from the locker area and jumped in his car and slammed the door behind him. He gunned the engine and it roared and spit gravel and he flew out of the parking lot and into traffic. He cut off two cars that had to swerve to avoid a head on crash.

Everyone in the locker room sat in stunned silence. Ike picked at the number on his jersey and Jeff reached down and tied his shoes again. The only sound was the hum of the heating ducts on the ceiling of the locker room. The heat from the room settled over the team and no one had the energy to fight against it. Finally, Coach Joe opened up the door to his office and he and the other coaches walked out. They walked pass the locker room like it was a morgue. Coach Joe leaned into the locker room and spoke quietly to the team.

"Gentlemen, it's time to get on the bus."

The team finished suiting up and grabbed their stuff and they got on the bus in silence and the coaches looked out the windows and didn't speak to each other and the bus left the parking lot and turned onto the main road and the team headed to Lawrence to keep their 36 game winning streak alive.

Lawrence Stadium was jam-packed. It was their homecoming night. This night, their fans were out of their minds. Lawrence was up, 24-21, with just under five minutes to play.

Jeff Tony was awful. His passes to Tim were either too high or too wide. Although Tim had managed to score a touchdown on a reverse and Quick Lou and Bill Bradner rumbled for scores, Lawrence picked off Jeff twice and capitalized on a rare Steve Staber fumble. Andy played in a fog. He was out of position most of the game or whiffed on easy tackles. He spelled Bill Bradner on one play and immediately fumbled a handoff.

Bobby was flagged for two unnecessary roughness calls. One was when he hit a Lawrence player with a wicked crack back block. The kid rolled into the Lawrence coaching staff. They fell into their bench like bowling pins. Coach Joe sent in Ike to take Bobby's place. When he walked off the field, he glanced up at Coach Joe. His coach stood on the sideline with folded arms and did not return Bobby's look. Bobby pushed pass his teammates and sat on the empty bench. He sprayed himself with water from a team bottle. His gold hair drooped and his soak-stained jersey stunk. He looked up into the stands and saw his sister looking down at him. Their eyes met and he held her gaze and finally let it go and turned back and watched the game that did not involve him anymore. He took off his helmet and dropped it on the bench. It made an eerie popping sound like a plastic ball that loses its air and deflates.

Chapter 36

The Great Steve Staber

The game looked out of reach for Beaumont, but then, Steve Staber took over. He rumbled six yards for a first down, then raced another eight on a toss sweep. He leapt to catch a high pass thrown as Jeff got slammed into the ground. Steve bowled over first one Lawrence tackler, and then another. Finally, he was pulled down by four Lawrence defenders. The clock showed 30 seconds and continued to tick down. Beaumont had the ball on Lawrence's 25 yard line. The team ran to the line of scrimmage so Jeff could spike the ball and stop the clock. Time was wasted in the mayhem. Ten seconds remained in the game and the Beaumont fans sensing another win, screamed for their team to pull off a miracle.

Donna remained quiet while the crowd around her went berserk. She saw the way the game unfolded. Beaumont looked awful and Lawrence played great. She saw Tim and Lou and Bill and the rest of the team gasp for air as Coach Joe sent in the final play of the game. She glanced over to see her brother put both is arms around the bench and lay his head back and look at the sky like there was no game going on. She knew better. This was one of the reasons Bobby didn't make friends. He looked like he didn't give a rat's ass about the game when she knew that his insides were tied up in knots and he was about to burst because things were not going in a way he could control. She looked back to the field and knew deep inside her, with everything she knew about herself and athletes and teams and just the way the world works sometimes, that Beaumont was not going to win this game.

Jeff Tony took the snap and dropped back a few feet and drilled a pass toward Tim that bounded through his hands just before he got jackknifed by a Lawrence defender. Tim flipped end over end and landed on his shoulder pads and helmet and sprawled on his back.

Seemingly out of nowhere, Steve Staber appeared. He reached down and somehow picked the fluttering ball out of the air, just inches from the ground. He made a quick motion toward the sideline, but a Lawrence player cut him off. Steve planted his left leg and stiff armed the Lawrence guy. He raced down the field with no blockers and five Lawrence players closed in. Steve saw that he could not get out of bounds. He lowered his shoulder and raced on. One Lawrence player bounced off. He lifted his knee and rammed another Lawrence player who dropped to the ground like a dead bird. Steve hunted down one Lawrence player, then another, and still another until finally, it seemed like the entire Lawrence team was on Steve's back. They ripped at the ball and grabbed his mud stained jersey. He carried the herd ever closer to the goal line.

Tim rolled over and looked up and saw the absolute fury that overcame Steve. He was like a wild animal fighting a pride of lions. With a final surge, Steve dove for the goal line. He was buried under the pile of Lawrence players. The officials moved in quickly and hauled players off the pile. When they finally dug through the mass of Lawrence plays and got to Steve, the officials looked to see where the ball landed. Steve clutched the ball in a death grip. The officials made the call. Steve Staber held the football just short of the goal line.

The Lawrence fans stormed the field. They were delirious as they swarmed the Lawrence players and coaches. They trampled a still prone Tim and shoved past Quick Lou and Bill Bradner, who both rocked on their knees in disbelief. Jeff Tony pulled turf out of his facemask and threw it across the field. Bobby got off the bench and grabbed his helmet and swung it over his head and slammed it into the ground. It bounced toward Coach Joe and bounced against his shin. Coach Joe didn't flinch. He looked out at the sea of Lawrence players and fans that jumped and danced and celebrated. He unfolded his arms and turned toward the bus and walked away. Beaumont's winning streak was over.

Chapter 37

Fast Food

That night, Donna sat with Tim at the downtown McDonald's. Normally, the place was packed. Parties got planned here, but not on this night. Some kids milled about, but they bought their cheeseburgers and fries and left quickly.

"Hurt?" Donna looked at Tim.

"Yes."

"Where?"

"Everywhere."

Tim looked down at his bruised shin and his gnarled hands. Donna ate a cold fry. Tim's burger remained untouched. He took a short pull from a chocolate shake. Eye black remained below his eyes from the game. Some of it smudged down his grimed-up face.

"What's next?" Donna handed a fry to Tim.

He took it and bit off the tip. It had no taste.

"We get ready for next week."

"And things will be fixed."

"No. I don't think so."

He stared at the untouched burger.

"No. I don't think they do get fixed. Not after this week."

Donna put her hand on top of Tim's. His hand had a deep, blue bruise from when he tried to throw a block and Bobby ran past and stepped on Tim's hand during the game. Donna gently rubbed the welt. She looked up and felt a cold wind blow into the restaurant and the door swung open. Bobby and Andy came in. They went to the counter and ordered something. Bobby turned and saw his sister sitting with Tim. Bobby left the counter and walked straight over and Andy followed a few steps behind. Bobby wore the same t-shirt he wore during the game that day. It stunk.

"Should have won that freaking game!"

Bobby yelled it loud enough for the cooks in the back of the restaurant to hear. He stood over Donna and Tim. Andy walked around and took a plastic chair and slid it over and he and sat next to Tim. The smell of booze and weed was thick.

"You're stoned." Donna looked hard at her brother. "You too, Andy. Think maybe that's why you guys lost?"

Bobby looked over at Tim and scowled and put his hands behind his head and leaned back and puffed out his chest.

"What do you think, Tim? We lost today because I get stoned?" Tim didn't look up at Bobby. But Tim did look at Andy. Their eyes met for just a second and then Andy turned away. Donna raised her voice. The remaining people in the restaurant stopped eating their food and turned in their seats and watched Donna erupt.

"Getting stoned and drunk doesn't help you win. It's not helping anything, you idiots!"

She stood up and shoved her brother. He stumbled back into a table. Leftover wrappers spilled onto the greasy floor. He regained his balance and walked toward his sister and shoved her back. She flew backwards and crashed into some plastic chairs and burger wrappers. She stuck out her arm and grabbed onto the table before she hit the floor. Tim jumped out of his chair and tried to keep Donna from hitting the ground, but there was no need. She regained her balance and bounced back up and ran at her brother like a wounded lion. Andy slid his chair backwards to get out of her way, but she ran through him and knocked him back and threw a punch that hit her brother square in the face. Bobby recoiled and grabbed his nose and there was lots of blood. He was dazed for a bit by his sister's punch. Donna leaped at her brother again and Tim tried to hold her back. She twisted and scratched at him and took another swing at Bobby that just missed his face. Tim held her from behind, but she twisted free again and with one hand, she grabbed Bobby's rank t-shirt and yanked him inches from her face.

"You lost tonight because your team's broke and it's broke because of you. And don't you ever put your hands on me again! You did it with dad. You had to. But never with me. You're still fighting that senseless war."

Andy stood next to Tim, and Donna let go of her brother and turned and grabbed Andy by the strings of his hoodie. She yanked the strings and the hoodie went tight around Andy's face and neck and she hissed at him.

"You're both fighting wars against people who are gone. Stop thinking the only reason both of you are smashed tonight is because you lost a freaking game. Deal with your problems or let them go!"

She shoved Andy and he took two quick steps backwards and seemed to deflate in front of everyone in the restaurant. Donna spun toward Tim and she shouted at him for the first time since they met.

"And what's happening in my family is none of your business, so don't be the good boyfriend and think I need to be saved. I don't!" Tim tried to take her hand, but she pulled it away like it was just burned. "And the three of you, it's just football. Dammit!"

She grabbed her coat and flung open the door and walked out and stepped onto the sidewalk. She started to run down the street and the traffic rolled past and the stop lights blinked and changed colors. Tim and Bobby and Andy stood there with their mouths agape and their fists clenched, and the few people left in the restaurant hurriedly finished their meals and cleaned up their own messes and left as quickly as they could.

Chapter 38

I Love You Guys

There was no state championship for the seniors that year. After the loss to Lawrence, Beaumont lost two more games before finally winning at home on Thanksgiving, beating a very poor Central Catholic team, 40-0. The Warriors walked off the muddy Memorial stadium field, but Steve Staber, Bill Bradner, and Lou Zarro remained behind. Their disappointment over how the season turned out was made bearable only by their deep friendship.

"I love you guys."

Quick Lou put his arms around Steve and Bill, and they pulled each other close and held on to each other and didn't mind crying with each other. Tim and Jeff waited for Steve and Bill and Lou and they walked off the field toward the lockers for the last time as teammates.

Bobby and Ike took off their home jerseys and walked to the lockers. They spoke to no one. Andy met his brothers at the gate. He played well today and he saw the pride in Zeke and Alex's eyes and he was grateful for that, but the season stunk and Andy knew it and he felt like he had let everyone down.

After the game when he finally left the locker room, Tim saw Donna standing by the gate. They had not spoken since the scene at the restaurant after they lost to Lawrence. His heart beat fast, but he tried to walk slowly towards her. She was tall and fair and her gold hair hung down to her shoulders. Her hands were tucked into the pockets of her blue jeans and the smallest of smiles formed on her face as Tim walked closer.

"Ok, so you guys finally played a good game. Maybe you don't suck."

She leaned against the fence and crossed one leg over the other.

"I thought you and I were over."

Tim walked closer.

"Who says we're not." She stepped toward him. "And it is still none of your business about my family."

"Of course. It's none of my business."

"I've missed you."

She leaned closer and touched her forehead to his.

"I've missed you."

Tim wrapped his arms around Donna and held her strong body and looked up and saw her deep, clear, blue eyes.

"Maybe we should talk."

She brushed her lips against his.

"Or something."

"Yeah, or something."

And they held each other because they had to and the maintenance guys tried to stamp down the sod and fix the field that got ripped up that season.

Chapter 39

Summer Burdens

Football and soccer began the first day of summer for the Beaumont Warriors. As they did every summer since they were in high school, Tim, Jeff, and Donna trained together. If anyone thought she didn't need to work out after she accepted her scholarship to North Carolina, it didn't show. She pushed herself relentlessly. If the plan was to do 10 sets of wind sprints, she made them all do 15. If Tim ran fifty pass routes, she made him do ten more, and she ran every pass pattern with him. She was the most complete athlete Tim had ever seen. And she never ran out of gas. Tim and Jeff began to lose steam after two hours in the heat of the afternoon. Donna took pity on them and signaled for them to get some water. They jogged over and drank down most of their water bottles and poured the remainder over their baking heads. Donna looked at them with scorn, but then grinned and she sat down on the bleachers and Tim and Jeff joined her. Jeff sat one row below Tim and Donna. He leaned back against the tin bleachers. Clearly, he had something on his mind. He turned around.

"Who do you think Coach Joe will pick for captains?"

Tim took some water left over in Donna's bottle and took another long swig and said nothing. Donna waited a few seconds and then broke the silence.

"I know who he should pick."

She looked at her boyfriend.

"I don't think I want that burden. It's too much."

Jeff punched Tim's shoulder and flung the question right back at her.

"No offense, Donna, but do you really think Bobby and Andy would make good captains?"

Jeff looked at Donna and expected her to punch him out, but she sat on the bleachers and looked away and didn't say anything. Tim answered his friend.

"They're the two best guys on the team and they've played varsity since sophomore year. They helped us win states. Maybe they should make captain."

"Is being good the only criteria for being a captain? We were lucky the last few years with Zeke and Alex and then Steve and Bill and Quick Lou. But Daniel was a captain until he bailed on us. There has to be more to a captain than just being the best on the team."

"Donna's the best on her soccer team and they made her captain. I don't think anyone would argue with that."

Tim leaned in and gave Donna a quick peck on the cheek. She slapped him away.

"Get away from me. You stink."

She laughed at Tim and punched his shoulder hard and he winced and laughed with her. Jeff jumped back in.

"Seriously, what if Coach picks them and they screw up? I don't think the team could take another year like the one we just had. I know I couldn't. I know I won't."

Jeff leaned over and tied a loose lace on his shoe and straightened back up and looked at Tim and then over to Donna. She surprised Jeff.

"I wouldn't pick Bobby, and he's my brother. I love him and I will forever, but he's too angry and he can't see past himself and what hurts him. At least Andy loves the team and loves the town. I don't think my brother is part of this place. It's almost like he's passing through and he's headed somewhere else so why bother with settling in."

Donna looked back at Jeff and then at Tim, and what she said sank in and the three of them sat on the broiling tin bleachers and the sun beat down and it felt like the heat of the summer would never break.

Chapter 40

Leaders and Followers

Tim and Donna ate pizza with Coach Joe. Tim finished his slice and excused himself to go to the bathroom. Donna was a fixture in their house over the summer. Where Coach Joe said little to his son, he was helpless to keep his mouth shut in front of Donna.

"I have to pick captains."

Coach Joe bit into a slice.

"This I know. Anyone in mind?"

"There's a few I've been thinking about."

"Do tell."

She leaned on her elbows and fixed her gaze on Tim's dad.

"There's Bobby and Andy, of course."

Donna shifted on the kitchen bench.

"And there's Tim."

She took a sip of soda.

"I'm not sure the team will understand if I pick my son."

Coach Joe crossed his legs and looked across the table at Donna.

"Have you talked to Tim?"

"No. I don't know what he'd say."

"Of course you don't since you haven't talked to him. I mean, Coach Joe?"

Tim came bounding down the stairs.

"What did I miss?"

"Your dad wants to ask you a question."

"I do?" Coach Joe smiled at Donna.

"Of course you do. Go ahead."

Coach Joe turned to his son.

"I'll just say it. Do you want to be a captain?"

Tim dreamt of this moment. But now it came to the point, and Tim hesitated. He sat quietly at the table. Donna turned toward Tim.

"You're worried about being captain because your dad's the coach."

Tim looked at her and then dropped his eyes.

"And Coach Joe, you're worried about Tim because he's your son."

Donna moved her eyes between both of them.

"I'd understand if you said no."

Coach Joe sat up straight for his son.

"But I wouldn't understand. You know your son well enough to know how strong he is and that he can take anything a captain needs to take."

Donna looked long at Coach Joe and then she turned and faced Tim.

"Tim, you've been a captain of the team for the last two years. You're just too stupid to realize it. Nothing's been easy for you. Being captain certainly won't be. The guys on the team don't need someone to be a leader because it's easy. They need a leader because they know it's hard."

"Son?" Coach Joe waited on Tim.

Donna looked deep into her boyfriend's eyes.

"Ok. I'll be captain."

He shook his dad's hand and grinned at Donna.

"What have you gotten me into?"

He kissed her in front of Coach Joe.

"So we're done eating pizza? For God's sake, let me have some of that!" She took the largest slice left in the box and then looked at the two of them. "Stop grinning, you two big dopes."

Coach Joe arrived at Andy's house. He walked up the familiar steps of the Jones' family porch and front door and let himself in. Mary Jones heard Coach Joe come in. She met him in the living room.

"Hello, Coach. Can I get you something to drink? I have water and soda, I think. A beer?"

"Some water would be fine."

Coach Joe took a seat on the sofa. Mary came in with a glass of ice water. The water droplets dripped down the glass as she handed him the drink.

"Thank you for stopping by. The boys so enjoy your visits. I appreciate everything you've done for them. It's been a tough few years, as you know."

Mary sat in the big chair her husband used to sit in. She tucked her legs under her dress and smiled. She relied on his visits, just like her boys. Zeke and Alex walked in from the back door. They were filthy from their work as part of the ground's crew at the local prep school. Scholarships didn't take away the family's need for money.

"Hello, Coach."

The boys stepped forward and Coach Joe got off the sofa. They shook hands vigorously. Zeke and Alex were full on men. They played well at college, and unlike too many of the guys on their teams, Zeke and Alex didn't skip class. Their mother wouldn't stand for it. Neither would Coach Joe. Their grades were solid.

"It's good to see you both. I'm glad you're here. Is Andy home?"

"He should be home any minute. He lugs kegs for the liquor store next to McDonald's downtown. Minimum wage, but he lifts each day, plus the kegs. He's jacked, Coach."

Both brothers beamed when they talked about Andy. They knew how much senior year meant. Now it was Andy's turn. Out back, a car door slammed and Andy bound up the stairs to the back door. He washed his hands at the kitchen sink and then stepped quickly into the living room.

"Coach!"

"Hello, Andy. I was wondering if I could speak with you for a minute."

Coach and Andy held their handshake. Mary, Zeke, and Alex turned to leave the room.

"I'd like you all to stay, if you don't mind."

Something in Coach Joe's voice reminded them of a visit he made a few summers ago when he came to speak to Zeke and Alex before their senior year. They all sat down in their family seats, long since worn from years of sitting together. Some good times. Some bad ones.

"Andy, I'd like you to be a captain this year." Coach Joe looked at Andy with clear eyes. "What do you say, son?"

It didn't take long for Andy to respond.

"I'll do my best, Coach. I promise."

"Well then. That's settled. I'll leave you to your family. Thank you for the water, Mary."

Coach Joe shook everyone's hands and let himself out. His car moved off into traffic. Every time he left, the Jones boys looked out the window until Coach Joe's car was out of sight. The older boys turned to their brother. Mary came close, pulling Andy with her. They hugged quietly, but the excitement of the moment soon took over. The four began to leap up and down.

"Captain Andy Jones of the Beaumont High School Warriors!" Zeke bellowed and the whole family jumped and laughed and cried and they drowned out the heavy drone of cars streaming by on the main road.

Coach Joe had another stop to make, but it would not be an easy visit. He drove into Bobby's family driveway. He walked to the front door and knocked. He waited for the door to open. He thought no one was home and turned to go back to his car when he heard footsteps. There was sound of multiple locks being released. Finally, the door opened.

Gwen Wilson stood in the door. She wore a work uniform from the local supermarket. Her hair was pulled up with a black hairband. She wore black, flat shoes. He noticed her eyes were sunk deep into her face. She smiled thinly.

"Coach Joe. Hello. Is Donna OK?"

"Oh yes, Mrs. Wilson. She's with Tim."

A brief look of relief passed across Gwen's face.

"They've become quite the pair."

She shifted her feet and let Coach Joe wait in the doorway.

"Mom. Let Coach in."

Bobby walked up behind his mother. He put two very large hands on her shoulders. Gwen's body relaxed.

"My goodness, my manners. I apologize, Coach Joe. Please, come in."

Bobby and his mom stepped to the side. Coach Joe walked into the kitchen. It was a small house. He looked around as he sat on one of the three kitchen chairs. The place was spotless. Appliances gleamed and the kitchen window was bright and clear as if someone had spent hours making sure it was without blemish. Coach Joe noticed the four locks on the kitchen door.

"I'd like to talk with Bobby about being a captain, Mrs. Wilson." Gwen sat down next to Coach Joe. Bobby leaned against the counter top. He stood with folded arms. His massive biceps burst through his t-shirt. His golden hair sparkled from the light of the sun through the window. His face looked like granite as he moved to take a seat next to his mom, across the table from Coach Joe.

"What do you think, son?"

Coach Joe looked directly into Bobby's eyes. Neither blinked. Coach Joe did not offer the captaincy to Bobby. He wanted to discuss it with him first. A gulf had to be bridged.

"Shouldn't Andy be captain?"

"I just left his house."

Coach Joe folded his hands on the table.

"So it would be Andy and me."

"That's right." He paused for a moment. "Tim too."

"Your son?" Bobby grunted.

Gwen looked from Bobby to Coach Joe. She saw the chasm between the two and she saw that it was very wide.

"That's right. Andy and you, and Tim. But you have to let the situation from last year with Daniel go, son. You need to stop fighting me on this. You're a natural leader, Bobby. The team listens to you. Andy listens to you."

Coach Joe sat back in the chair.

"I don't know, Coach. I'm playing. That's for sure. But some of your rules, Coach. I'm not seeing them."

"They're the team rules. If you can't live by them, don't be captain."

Bobby's eyes shifted away from Coach Joe. He wanted this. Probably more than anything. He imagined wearing his team letter jacket with a big "D" on one breast and a captain's "C" on the other. He would be the leader of the team. He would be someone other than the son of someone who beat his wife. The man Bobby had almost killed with his bare hands. Gwen reached over and put her hand on Bobby's forearm.

"Be captain for this man, Bobby. He's a good man. A good man." Gwen leaned toward her son. She took her hand off his forearm and then placed both of her hands on his shoulders. She rubbed them gently and Bobby's stone face began to relax and the muscles at the back of his neck softened. After a few moments, he spoke to Coach Joe.

"I'll be your captain." Bobby turned to his mom.

He saw the old welt marks on her upper arms. And then he looked up at her and saw a smile she seldom showed. It lit him up.

"Good. I'll expect your best, son. Every day. You can be a fine leader, Bobby. Just let things go."

"Fine."

He stood up with Coach Joe. They shook hands and looked into each other's eyes. Coach Joe released the handshake and let himself out the door. He got in his car and drove off. Gwen Wilson stood and reached up to hug her son and the two held each other in the quiet of their small kitchen.

Chapter 41

Seniors

Preseason came to an end for the Beaumont Warriors. The assistant coaches finished the wind sprints with the team. Everyone dripped with sweat. Their bodies ached as they ran one more sprint. Tim finished ahead of the rest of the team, by far. Bobby and Jeff raced side by side. Neither let the other win. Andy ran with the rest of the team and encouraged the newbies.

"That's it. I'm done. I can't take any more." Ike flopped to the ground. His back screamed in agony and his hamstrings burned. "Please, Coach Joe!"

His pleas cracked up the rest of the team. Even Coach Joe smiled. Ike was the team clown. But Ike was right. The team had had enough.

"Gentlemen. Bring it in."

In spite of their utter fatigue, the team ran to Coach Joe.

"There's been talk about the win streak being broken last year. Bad things happen to good teams. You can only control your now. Starting this Friday night, we will begin our now. The decisions you make today will carry you the entire season. Bobby, Andy, Tim. Go off together and set goals for the team. The rest of you. Break it off."

The Warriors shouted, "1, 2, 3, Team!" They took off their helmets and ran in unison toward the lockers. Coach Joe and his assistants walked together. It was a long week with intense heat for most of the practices. Now the coaches headed in to prepare their game plan for their first game just a week away.

Bobby, Andy, and Tim walked off toward the shade of a single maple tree at the far end of the practice area, not too far from the gates to Memorial Field. Tim took a knee. Bobby stood over him. Andy stood slightly behind.

"I think we could be really good this year."

Tim stood back up and faced Bobby and Andy.

"Well, before we get into that crap, I'm letting you know right now I'm partying this season. Andy, too. Right Andy?"

Andy moved slightly to Bobby's right. He nodded his head slightly in agreement. The sun set directly behind Andy, and at that moment, it was hard for Tim to see his friend.

"And you're not saying a damn thing to your dad. Not a stinking thing. We've been partying for all three years of football. We've won plenty. I'm not stopping just because I'm your old man's captain."

Bobby turned to face Andy and he nodded twice more.

"I'm with him."

Tim stared at Andy for a long time.

"There it is." Bobby looked at Tim. "I'm having a party tonight. Three kegs. You come if you want, but you keep your mouth shut about it."

Tim looked back and forth between Bobby and Andy.

"That's it? You're screwing the team. You know that, right? And you're screwing yourself. What am I supposed to do? He's my dad. He's our coach. I just shut up, right?"

"That's exactly right. You've known about this for years. You've never missed a party. You had your chance to tell your dad and you didn't. You have your reasons." Bobby took a quick step toward Tim. "So you keep your mouth shut, and we'll be fine." He gave Tim a quick shove and Tim fell back and banged into the maple tree. Bobby walked backwards in a taunting strut. His eyes bore into Tim's before he turned and strode off. Andy looked quickly at Tim and then turned and loped after Bobby.

Tim watched Bobby and Andy stride off as he slid down the length of the maple tree. He sat in the shade and found it very hard to breathe. He lay there with his feet apart and looked at the football field that was so much a part of his life and the field was dark and green and long and wide and he was completely alone and the sun set slowly behind the empty stadium.

Chapter 42

Swinging Helmet

Beaumont opened the season at home against Pentucket Regional. Coach Joe started Andy at running back, and in a surprise move, moved Tim to running back as well. He wanted Tim's sprinter's speed to be a compliment to Andy's tough running style. Jeff Tony started at quarterback, with Ike at split end.

With the score tied 14-14 late in the game, Tim took a toss sweep around left end. Andy threw a brutal block and flattened the Pentucket defensive end. Tim shifted gears and raced down the sideline. Bobby ran interference, knocking down first one Pentucket defender and then another. Tim deftly followed Bobby's blocks with one hand on Bobby's back. Tim guided Bobby toward the last Pentucket player that stood between Tim and the goal line. Just as the safety moved in for the tackle, Tim shoved Bobby from behind and hurtled him into the legs of the Pentucket defender. Tim cut away from the pile and ran the remaining thirty yards for the game winning touchdown. As Bobby pulled himself away, he ran up and over the chest of the helpless Pentucket kid. Their sideline screamed at the officials who somehow missed the dirty play. Two players from the sideline tried to get at Bobby as he taunted them with his arms outstretched, beckoning them to try and take him on.

The game ended and the handshake line formed. Some of the Pentucket players and coaches seethed from the cheap play of Bobby. He extended a hand to the player who he mangled a few minutes earlier. The kid slapped Bobby's hand away and drove his helmet into Bobby's chest. A Beaumont assistant coach jumped in to stop the fight, but Bobby grabbed the face mask of the Pentucket player and twisted it in a jerk and pulled off the helmet. He threw the helmet toward the Pentucket cheerleaders who dove out of the way except for one who wasn't paying attention. Bobby's helmet bounced over the turf and hit her square in the stomach. She flopped over and cheerleaders rushed to her aid and parents came out of the stands to help. Hell broke out. One Pentucket player tackled Bobby from behind. Another player jumped into the melee and grabbed Bobby's golden hair and hauled him down from behind and dragged him across the field, just before Andy jumped in to rescue his friend. Andy got cold cocked for his trouble. He swooned and fell over dizzy and tried to get back up, but another Pentucket player shoved him down and four more jumped on top of Andy and showered him with blows to the head and gut. Tim saw Andy go down and he raced from the back of the handshake line to try to help his friend. He drove his shoulder pad into one Pentucket kid and sent him sprawling. Tim ripped off his own helmet and swung it like a medieval weapon. Two Beaumont coaches raced in and separated Tim from the crazed Pentucket players, but not before Tim took the meat of his palm and drove it into the helmet of one of Andy's attackers. The kid dropped like a rock and Tim grabbed on to Andy and pulled him back toward the safety of the Warrior sideline. The refs tried to restore order and police tried to hold back fans from both teams from killing each other.

When the fights were finally over and calm restored, Coach Joe tried to find the Pentucket coach. He didn't have to look hard because the livid Pentucket coach jogged over to Coach Joe and screamed in his face.

"That was bush league! Wilson ran over my kid when the play was done. Then he taunted us as he ran down the sideline. I'm filing a complaint with the conference!"

His face was purple. Coach Joe extended his hand to calm the coach, but the Pentucket coach was having none of it.

"Your team never plays this way. You better reign in Wilson. That wasn't the only time he played cheap. My guys said he was like that all game."

"I'm very sorry, coach. I'll make sure it never happens again." The Pentucket coach calmed down a bit and the two shook hands and moved off. The Beaumont assistants herded the Warriors toward the locker room. Coach Joe followed. He looked to find Tim but could not see him in the swirl of Warrior players and fans. His walking slowed. The lights of the field began to blur and his heart raced. He stopped and tried to regain control of his breathing. As usual, everyone gave Coach Joe space after a game. So no one saw him bend over and put his hands on his knees. In a few seconds, the dizziness passed and Coach Joe's heart rate dropped back to near normal. He stood back up and carefully looked to make sure no one noticed. Seeing his son fight a crowd of Pentucket kids was almost too much for even Coach Joe to bear.

Chapter 43

Back Time

The locker room was in a frenzy over the big win, but probably more so because of the brawl. Players whooped and high fived and slapped each other on the back. In the craziness, Andy turned and bumped into Tim. Andy remembered the sucker punch he got at the end of the game. He remembered seeing Tim dive into the pile of Pentucket players and fight like a wild dog, even though there were five of them. Andy put his hand on Tim's shoulder and the two smiled at each other for the first time in quite a while.

"Thanks for getting me out of that mess. I find myself on the ground and look up and all I see is this crazy kid swinging his helmet. You could have got yourself killed."

Tim put his hand on Andy's shoulder and left it there for a bit and looked deep into Andy's eyes.

"We're champions together. We're champions forever. Isn't that what you said to me a few years ago? Nothing changes that, ever. I'm not sure we like each other anymore, but we'll always love each other."

Andy looked back at Tim and remembered a night a few years ago and the state championship and the fire. Andy remembered the last day of pre-season a few weeks ago and how he went along with Bobby and how he didn't really want to but knew he couldn't stand up to Bobby. Andy knew what it had done to Tim.

"I don't know what to say. I wish things were like they used to be."

"I think we both know we can't go back to that. Things have changed too much."

Tim took in a very deep breath and looked around at the rest of the guys. They looked like a perfect team, but it was just a mirage and both Tim and Andy knew it.

"People have changed too much. But I'll always be there for you, and I hope you'll always be there for me."

"Of course I will," Andy said to Tim.

Tim took his hand off of Andy's shoulder and he went back to his locker and took off the rest of his soaked uniform and athletic tape and eye black and he wished he and Andy could go back to the way things were. He pulled off his football pants and threw them in a dirty pile in his locker and looked up and saw Bobby looking at him, and Tim knew that things had changed just too much.

Chapter 44

Bottles and Stones

That night, the party at Ike's raged. The boom of the music filled the night. On the front lawn, Bobby chugged two beers back to back. Many of his classmates egged him on. He took a long drag from a joint he held in his left hand. He held it in and finally let it out in a deep exhale. He swayed and Ike and Andy kept him from falling.

Donna and Tim sat in her car not far down the street. They saw Bobby sway and his friends catch him. They heard cheering and laughing through the hard-driving music.

"Well, I guess now it's a party."

She looked over the steering wheel at her brother. Tim put his feet up on the dashboard.

"Yes, I'd say it is."

Tim frowned as he saw Bobby chug another beer. Andy stood near Bobby along with some other partiers. He hoisted up his own beer and downed it in three swallows. He reared back and threw the empty bottle into a nearby stand of trees. Ike grabbed three more beers and handed them out.

"You know you can't do anything about this."

Donna put her hand through the back of Tim's hair.

"You're right. I can't."

He looked out at the party.

"Everything about what I see tonight stinks."

Donna watched her brother take another long drag from the joint.

"And you can't do anything for your brother."

Tim turned toward Donna.

153

"I've tried." She put her head on Tim's shoulder. He put his arm around her. "He's broken," she whispered.

"I think your brother is taking me down with him."

Tim placed his left leg over her right one. They sat quietly. They no longer looked at Bobby and Andy and Ike or the party.

"What am I supposed to do? The drinking and the drugs are ruining the team. I can't tell my dad about what happened with me and Bobby and Andy."

"You're right," Donna said. You can't tell your dad."

"I'm not a captain. Bobby and Andy ended it for me on the first day of practice."

"No. You're not." Donna spoke softly.

"I hate it."

Tim looked at Donna.

"You might not be able to hold this together, Tim."

"There's nothing I can do. Nothing at all."

Tim breathed slowly.

"Nothing about this is fair, but you can't quit on this."

"I know, but your brother doesn't need to play like an animal. He's too good."

"He doesn't think so," she said. "It's an act. He could be the best guy on the field and it still wouldn't be good enough. Not for him."

"He's one of the best players I've ever seen. I'd tell him if I thought he might listen to me."

"Yes. I know you would." She turned to face Tim. "He just keeps fighting everyone."

"Sometimes I hate your brother."

"I know you do. But you don't know him."

"Maybe you can tell me. What happened to you and your mom and Bobby and your dad?"

"I can't go back to that. It almost broke my mom and Bobby. It might break me. I can't talk about it."

"I understand. When you're ready, I'll listen. I don't know if I can help, but I'll listen."

"I can't look at this party anymore and I can't look at my brother getting drunk and stoned. I can't look at what he's doing to himself and I hate what this is doing to you."

Donna slammed her fist down on the steering wheel.

"Then let's not stay and torture ourselves. Let's get out of here. I want something to eat anyway. You know I'm always hungry." Tim smirked at Donna and made a thumb gesture like they should leave. Donna slid back behind the steering wheel and turned on the ignition and they drove away from the party and their car slid past where Bobby sat with his back against a tree away from the other partiers. Donna and Tim saw that he was all alone in the dark.

The Beaumont Warrior game against Tewksbury was a disaster. They returned a veteran team and it showed. Beaumont was able to move the ball down the field only to have fumbles or interceptions end their drives. Tewksbury scored three times late in the second half and stunned the Warriors, 21-10. Coach Joe met the reporters immediately after the game. His face was drawn and his eyes sallow.

"Tewksbury is a fine team. They deserved the win and I wish them the best."

"Coach Joe. Your team looked sluggish tonight. Can you tell us about this? Some of my sources say there are problems between players on the team. Can you comment on this?"

Reporters clicked their pens and wrote on their yellow pads of paper.

"We lost to a better team. The loss is on me, and that's all. Thank you for your time."

Coach Joe nodded once and walked pass the reporters and left them to scribble their notes and whisper between each other that the Warriors weren't losing games because they didn't have talent. They sensed that something dark had taken over the team.

Chapter 45

Chasm

After the game, the Warriors finished changing in their locker room. No one said much other than Ike.

"No worries, gentlemen. There's plenty of season left to play. We got Wilmington next week. They're dead meat."

Ike laughed, and some of his teammates murmured in agreement. Not everyone was so polite.

"Shut the hell up." Andy threw down a towel. His back was bruised, and his left leg had a gash down the length of his calf. "That's four losses in our last six games. We suck." He looked at Tim who gazed out from his locker. "We had nothing tonight."

"You mean you had nothing tonight." Bobby leered at Andy. "You whiffed on tackles. You played like a pussy. You all did."

"Bull. We all played like crap." Andy stood up and stepped toward Bobby. "We lost. You included."

Tim felt sick. He tried to step between Bobby and Andy.

"Take it easy. We'll get it back next week. We can take Wilmington."

Bobby pushed Andy away and stared at Tim.

"And you can stick that rah-rah crap up your ass, daddy's boy," Bobby barked at Tim.

The other Beaumont players turned and stared. The rift on the team was laid bare. Tim looked over the edge of a dark, deep abyss.

"And you can screw yourself, Wilson."

He charged at Bobby. He jumped over a bench and slammed Bobby into a locker. Bobby crashed against the metal and his breath burst out and he grunted but grabbed Tim by his shirt and bench pressed him off, and with his elbow, he bashed Tim's jaw. Ike and Jeff tried to pull the two apart. Bobby threw a late punch that grazed off Tim's head. Tim took a fistful of Bobby's hair and yanked it down toward the floor. Bobby screamed and bent Tim's fingers back until he let go of his sweaty, golden locks. Jeff jumped in and pulled Tim away, and Ike held onto Bobby like he was a wildcat. The team watched the fight and stood like voiceless statues.

"The day you got here, I knew you wrecked the team. You should have stayed in California!" Tim screamed out.

This time, it was Bobby's turn to charge. He elbowed Ike in the gut and broke free. He hit Tim square on the jaw with his fist and drove him over the bench. He straddled Tim and threw punch after punch, most blocked by Tim's arms and elbows. Tim drove his knee into Bobby's crotch and flipped him over. Bobby howled in agony and rolled away, holding his groin with both hands. Tim lay on the floor and his chest heaved up and down and he tried to get some air back into his lungs. They were exhausted. The fight was done.

Andy stood by himself in the back of the locker room. He watched the whole fight, but didn't jump in to stop it because he knew he couldn't stop it. It had to play out, but he felt like he was stuck between two avalanches crashing toward each other from very different mountains. Andy turned away and grabbed his stuff and let himself out of the back door to the locker room and he walked home by himself in a night devoid of any light.

Chapter 46

Blocking Drill

On the second day of practice for Beaumont the following week, the running backs and the linebackers squared off in a blocking drill. Tim lined up at his running back spot and Bobby grabbed a blocking shield with the other linebackers. Coach Joe addressed the team. It had been a long week for him and his team was either going to pull itself out of this dark pit or they were going to get swallowed up and never get out.

"Last week is over. Wilmington is our focus. Put it behind you and focus just on this one drill. Just this one drill. And then we go to the next drill and we get better and we get ready for Wilmington."

The girls' soccer practice was just finishing up. Donna stood with some friends and watched the drill.

The drill began and Jeff Tony handed the ball off to Andy. When the ball was snapped, Tim burst out of his stance and hurtled toward Bobby. The two managed to avoid each other all week. Not so today. Tim launched himself into Bobby. Coach Joe blew his whistle quickly, but the force of his son's hit caught Bobby off guard. He ended up sprawled onto his back. He leapt up to charge Tim. Andy jumped in and held back Bobby. Coach Joe watched, arms folded with his whistle held in his mouth.

"Jesus. It's a drill, for God's sake."

Bobby seethed as Tim moved away. Tim jogged back to his position.

"Run it again, Jeff."

Tim got back into his stance. Bobby grabbed the blocking dummy and dug his feet into the ground like a bull at a bull fight.

"Ok. Tim, we'll run it again." Jeff barked out the signals.

Tim fired out of his stance and drove his helmet deep into Bobby's chest. This time Bobby was ready and drove back against Tim's onslaught. The two battled like rams on a mountaintop. Their helmets locked together as they tried to disengage. The whistle dropped from Coach Joe's lips. Tim finally twisted away from Bobby and ran back to his spot. He yelled at the top of his voice.

"Again!"

Andy saw Tim's shoulder pads heave up and down and Andy knew that the battle between Tim and Bobby could not go on much longer. Andy held the football in one hand and watched this battle that didn't seem to have ended in the locker room after the game against Tewksbury.

"Ok, but this is the last time. Take it easy, Tim."

Jeff sounded out the cadence once more. Players in other drills came over. They saw the battle and were astonished at the violence. Across the practice fields, the girls on the soccer team watched. Donna held two hands to her mouth.

When Tim drove out of his stance, Bobby dropped his blocking shield. Both players hit so hard, they flew off each other and landed square on their backsides. The collision took the air out of both of them and they sat in utter exhaustion. Coach Joe seemed impressed with the effort and completely misread what he just witnessed.

"You play like this on Friday night against Wilmington, you can't lose. You two bring out the best in each other." Coach Joe nodded toward Tim and Bobby. "We're coming together as a team after a tough loss last week. I can see it. I'm proud of both of you. That's enough for today. All right, Jeff, break them off." Coach Joe turned and walked off toward the locker area and his assistants walked just behind.

Donna walked by herself toward the lockers. She watched Tim and Bobby glare at each other and she knew that whatever was rotting between her brother and Tim had just become so much worse.

Chapter 47

A Pass in the Mist

Beaumont's game against the Wilmington Eagles was a battle from the very start. Both teams scored early. Andy made a long touchdown run and Jeff threw a short pass to Ike who broke two tackles and galloped into the end zone for a 14-0 Beaumont lead at halftime. In the second half, Wilmington battled back as a steady rain began to fall. They scored two touchdowns and kicked a field goal to take a 17-14 lead. Beaumont got the ball back with 1:30 to go in the fourth quarter. Two passes to Ike and one to Andy were knocked down by diving Eagle defensive backs. It was fourth and ten from Beaumont's own 25-yard line. Coach Joe sent in a play. "Short left, 29 toss sweep." The play was designed for Andy to get the first down and get out of bounds and stop the clock. There were now 16 seconds left in the game. Tim heard the play and he stepped toward Jeff in the huddle and put one hand on his shoulder pad.

"Change the play and give me the ball."

Jeff stood in the huddle and didn't know what to do. He looked at the rest of the team.

"Change the play, Jeff. Give me the ball. I'll get the first down," Tim spoke firmly and confidently.

"Run the stinking play Coach Joe called, Jeff," Bobby commanded. "It's Andy's ball."

Tim turned his body toward Bobby.

"No. I'll make it! Here's the new play. Short right, 28 toss. Andy, take out the defensive end. Ready, break!"

Jeff did not argue and the team ran to the line of scrimmage. Neither did Ike, or Andy.

"Damn it!" Bobby got in his stance and glanced back one more time at Tim.

Tim went in motion to his right. The ball was snapped, and Jeff pivoted. He tossed the ball out in front of Tim who sped up and caught the ball and tucked it away in his right armpit. Wilmington's best player tried to cut off Tim before he could get to the sideline, but Andy raced toward the Eagle and cut his legs out from under him. Tim leapt pass the sprawling defender and turned up field and aimed for the first down marker on the Wilmington sideline. Two Eagle defenders met Tim full on as he dove for the first down. All three players somersaulted into the Wilmington coaches and players. The official raced in and spotted the ball on the 36 yard-line.

"First down!" he shouted, and the chains moved upfield.

Eleven seconds remained on the clock. Beaumont used their last time out. They were exhausted, and they took their time as they walked toward the sideline. Coach Joe waited for them and his heart raced, and his breathing was short. He waited a few seconds to recover before he talked to his team. The assistant coaches thought Coach Joe was thinking up some magic play. They were wrong. Coach Joe was as exhausted as his team.

"We have time for one more play. Great block, Andy. But I thought I called that play for you." The team remained silent. "Well, nice run, Tim. OK, you and Andy are gassed. Let's run Gun, 61 Hail Mary. Tim, you run a short sideline square out. Ike, you have gas left in your tank. You run a deep fade down the sideline. Get beyond the Wilmington defensive backs. You offensive linemen, give Jeff enough time to help him make the throw. Gentlemen, this is it."

The Beaumont players jogged back to their huddle. Tim put a hand on Ike's shoulder pad.

"Ike, you switch with me. I'll take split end. You run my short out. I'm going deep."

"Jesus, Tim. Coach said you're gassed. Let Ike run the deep route." Bobby stood with his hands on his hips and faced Tim. "Jesus."

"No. Ike, you make the switch. Jeff, just throw it as far as you can. I'll catch it. Ready, break!"

The team ran up to the line and got set for the last play of the game.

From the stands, Donna saw the commotion in the huddle. This was the second play she saw the team argue in the huddle. Of course, Tim and her brother were in the middle of it. She wasn't surprised when Beaumont broke their huddle and Tim lined up as the wide receiver and Ike at running back.

"Damn," she said to no one in particular as she watched the Warriors line up for the last play of the game.

Coach Joe stood a few steps behind the sidelines. The formation was correct, but he saw Tim line up at split end and Ike at Tim's normal running back position. He took a step closer to the sideline and folded his arms and watched and the tiniest smile formed on his face.

Jeff stood in shotgun formation. He scanned the field. Wilmington had most of their defenders way back to try and stop the Hail Mary. Their coach screamed from the sideline to not let any Beaumont receiver get behind them.

Jeff called out the cadence and took the snap. He dropped back a full five more steps to set up. He needed to give his receivers time to sprint down the field. He looked to his left and saw Ike covered. Jeff now had only one option. He took a step forward and heaved the football as far as he could. Two Wilmington defensive linemen crashed into Jeff and planted him backwards. The ball arced into the rain in a perfect spiral. His face was squashed into the mud by a Wilmington player, so Jeff never saw his pass fall back to earth.

Tim raced at an angle toward the sideline and then straight toward the end zone, 54 yards away. About 30 yards downfield, Tim felt his left calf cramp. He was completely dehydrated. He played every play on offense and defense. He willed himself to relax his overtaxed calf muscle and somehow it did. He flew downfield and drew level with the Eagle defensive backs.

They were stunned by Tim's speed. They tried to keep up, but Tim raced past them. They ran after him and saw Tim adjust his speed as the ball fell out of the rain.

Tim leapt. He extended his hands and felt the slick leather of the ball. One of the Wilmington defenders stumbled trying in vain to keep up with Tim. The other two did not. They launched themselves into the air, but they were too late. Tim corralled the ball and quickly tucked it away. The two Eagles dove on Tim's shoulder pads and stripped and punched and clawed at the ball.

Tim drove his knees and churned on. His left leg cramped again, and he felt the overwhelming weight of the Wilmington defenders. They grabbed and yanked on his uniform and Tim began to stumble.

Donna froze as she watched the ball fall from the sky and into Tim's outstretched hands. Her heart almost stopped as she watched Tim run away from one defender and haul the other two towards the goal line.

With his last ounce of strength, Tim dove. He collapsed in a heap with the Wilmington defenders on top of him. A lone official ran toward the pile of players. There was a moment of complete silence and the crowds from both towns rose to their feet.

The official pulled both Wilmington players off of Tim. In the same motion, Tim took the football in one hand and raised it up. The official raised both arms above his head and yelled "Touchdown!" The Beaumont fans went nuts.

The entire Beaumont team raced toward the end zone. They crashed into Tim as he picked himself off the ground. The football remained held above Tim's helmet as he was knocked backwards and onto the ground. He felt the weight of his team on top of him and he found that he couldn't breathe.

Andy saw his teammate trying to get air into his lungs. He pushed off celebrating Beaumont players and grabbed Tim's chin strap and snapped it off and pulled Tim's helmet over his ears.

"Let the man breathe, for God's sake!"

Air flowed back into Tim's lungs. His teammates pounded his shoulder pads and whacked him on the back. One player accidentally kicked Tim in the calf muscle and Tim screamed in pain. Andy helped Tim toward the sidelines. The official trailing the play threw a flag.

"Too many men on the field. Five-yard penalty at the spot of the kickoff."

Coach Joe ran out to confront the official.

"How can you throw a flag on a play like that? There's no way my boys could have stayed on the sideline."

Coach Joe's assistants saw that the official was about to throw another penalty flag, so they pulled Coach Joe away and back toward the sideline.

Finally, Tim and Andy reached Coach Joe and he put an arm around his son.

"That was pretty good. You'll have to tell me what play I ended up calling," Coach Joe laughed, and Tim managed to smile in spite of his exhaustion.

Andy shook Coach Joe wildly.

"Your son won the game, Coach!"

Another official ran over to the sideline.

"Coach Joe. Get the rest of your players on the field or I'm throwing another flag. Delay of game. Let's go, Coach Joe!"

"Come on, you dinks. We have a game to win!"

Bobby pulled both Tim and Andy back onto the field. Tim staggered and tried to line up with the kickoff team as he neared the point of passing out.

Beaumont lined up for the kickoff. Ike ran up and squib kicked the ball and it skidded across the wet turf. A Wilmington player picked it up and raced to his left toward his own sideline. But this was a trick play. Their fastest kid ran in the opposite direction and took the ball from his teammate. It was a reverse, and it stunned the Beaumont defenders. The Wilmington kid raced for the Beaumont sideline.

Donna held onto one of her friends as the ball squirmed toward the Wilmington kid. She stood in shock as she saw the reverse take shape and she saw the Beaumont players fall for the trick. When the Eagle player took the reverse and headed at full speed in the opposite direction, Donna could see that the Eagle player could score. She brought her hands to her mouth and shouted, "No!" The rest of the crowd realized what Donna saw. They screamed with her. Beaumont's heroic win was about to be snatched away.

When Ike kicked the ball, Tim stayed back. He saw the Wilmington kid streak toward his own sideline and then slow down to hand the ball to his teammate. It was a reverse and he saw his team had been completely faked out. Tim planted his foot and gave chase, but there was just about no more gas in his tank. He tried to cut off the Wilmington kid. The Eagle player shifted his weight and cut back across open field. Tim tried to grab the player's uniform, but it was too wet, and Tim had no more strength. He slipped on the wet grass and fell in the mud and the Wilmington player raced toward the goal line.

Out of nowhere, Bobby appeared. He saw the reverse too late, but he did not give up on the play. He lowered his chin and sprinted. He saw Tim slow the Wilmington kid up just a bit. With a full dive, Bobby tripped up the foot of the Wilmington player. For a moment, it seemed like the kid would keep his balance, but inertia worked against him. His center of gravity was too far forward. He put his hand down to keep himself from falling, but it was a failed effort. He took a few more strides and finally fell forward into the mud and slid head first 10 yards from the end zone. The game was over. The Beaumont players charged onto the field and this time the officials threw no penalty flag. The Warriors swarmed Bobby and lifted him off the ground and pounded his shoulder pads. He let out a victory howl. Final score, Beaumont, 20, Wilmington 17.

The players from both teams set up in two lines to shake hands. Andy walked behind Bobby just to make sure he didn't say anything stupid. The Wilmington coach pulled Tim aside.

"That was a hell of a catch, young man."

Tim shook the coach's hand.

"Thank you, sir."

He let go of the coach's hand and joined his teammates as they ran toward their team buses.

Donna met Tim in the parking lot as the team got on the bus. She hugged him even though he was soaking wet. Tim grinned sheepishly, and she slapped him on the backside as he climbed onto the screaming busload of Warrior players. Then Donna walked over to her brother and pulled him close and hugged him hard.

"You saved the game with that tackle. You didn't quit on the play. I'm proud of you." Bobby looked at his sister and smiled and kissed her cheek and some of his sweat dripped onto her face and she slapped him away.

"God, Bobby! Get away from me."

She slapped her brother's backside, just like she did to Tim. Bobby ran up the stairs of the bus and yelled and cheered with the rest of the team.

The team celebrated when they got back to Beaumont and filed into their locker room. When they got inside, Tim grabbed Bobby from behind and spun him around.

"You saved our asses."

Tim looked stone-faced at Bobby and then smacked him on his soaking-wet game jersey. Bobby looked at Tim and didn't smile.

"Yeah, well, nice catch. That was bullshit changing the plays, though. But pretty good bullshit." Bobby extended a hand and Tim shook it. "Now get the hell away from my locker."

Bobby smiled and shoved Tim away. Tim smiled back at Bobby and made his way back to his own locker. When he got there, he was mobbed by Andy and Jeff and even Ike.

"You just wouldn't go down! You carried three guys on your back. Jesus!"

Ike picked Tim off the ground in a sweaty bear hug.

"It was just two. But thanks, Ike. Now put me down, you stinking animal."

Ike dropped Tim back to the ground and grabbed him by the face and kissed him on the lips and screamed and laughed and took off his towel and whipped Tim on the butt. He ran off naked and jumped on other players. The locker room was in complete chaos. Andy came over and sat with his friend.

"Good Lord, man! Ike just kissed you on the lips. Jesus! I love him, but I don't think he could have made that play. I think I could have made that first down until you changed the play, you bastard." He laughed and put his arm on Tim's shoulder. The two slumped back into their lockers. "You made the right call."

"We weren't going to lose. There was no way."

Tim put his arm around Andy.

"You're right. We weren't going to lose!"

The locker room was electric. Finally, Tim took a deep breath and grabbed his helmet and jumped up on the bench and pulled Andy up and they sang, and they jumped, and the locker room rocked in a haze of victory.

Coach Joe sat in his office. It was a big win. He let his assistants go home to their families. They worked hard all week and they needed the break.

He leaned back in his arm chair. His temples throbbed. He felt the office spin. Sweat formed on his forehead. He concentrated on his breathing and felt it slowly come under control. He wiped the sweat off his forehead and the spinning room slowly came back to normal. He sat there for a bit and the fit of fatigue passed. This was the third time this season that he felt this kind of extreme exhaustion. He thought about his son and the last play of the game and how the team mobbed him, and Coach Joe laughed first quietly, then hard. His laughing ebbed, and he turned off the light near his desk and the room became dark and he tried to rest.

Chapter 48

Arrested Development

That night, Tim and Donna decided they wanted to go to Ike's party. It was raucous, and again, there was plenty of beer and dope. Some kids paired off and made out. Others danced to the heavy metal that blared from Ike's speakers. Donna and Tim joined the dancing. They jumped to the beat with their arms around each other and it was a great night.

Around 1:00 am, some neighbors had enough with the noise and called the police. A couple cruisers rolled up in front of Ike's. Four cops got out. Joints were tossed and beers drained. Ike met them by his front door.

"Beaumont's finest. Welcome! Come inside and join the party." Ike laughed and shook their hands. They cops were not amused.

"Don't you think this party has gone on long enough, Ike?" He was well known to the Beaumont police. "Maybe you should send your friends home. That way, we won't have to go through your house and find anything interesting. Are your parents home tonight, Ike?"

"Of course, they're home. They turned in early."

Ike stepped outside. He yelled to get everyone's attention.

"Party's over. We're getting shut down. Please leave in an orderly fashion."

The kids at the party laughed and began to leave. Tim and Donna heard Ike and the police and they came up out of the basement and tried to leave. A police officer met them at the door and put his hand up for them to stop.

"Your dad know you've been drinking, son? Ain't drinking against Coach Joe's rules?"

Donna stepped toward the cop.

"He doesn't drink and he doesn't smoke and neither do I."

Donna looked at the cop. Bobby came up from the basement with Andy close behind.

"No, they do not. I can attest to that. Trust me, you're looking at two of the straightest kids in town!"

Bobby slurred some of his words as he walked toward the police officers.

"You seem to have had a few beers. Bobby Wilson, right? And you're one of the Jones boys. Andy, is that right? Well, that was a hell of a game I saw this afternoon."

One of the other cops shined a light in Bobby's face and then moved it quickly to Andy's.

"Chief, I think these fine gentlemen have had more than a few beers tonight."

The Chief looked closely at the two captains.

"Is that right? You boys drink too much tonight?"

"They're fine. We'll take care of them."

Tim put his hand on Andy's shoulder. Donna put her hands on Bobby and kept her brother from falling over.

"No, we're fine, officers. Truly fine." Bobby moved to shake the chief's hand, but he stumbled slightly and bumped one of the other cops. "My apologies. Please, let's shake."

Once more, Bobby tried to find the hand of the chief. He missed again, this time falling into the chief's arms.

"You're drunk, son."

"Maybe just a little." Bobby burped.

The chief was tired of the display.

"I think you should come with us. You too, Jones. Cool off at the station. You can leave in the morning."

"I'm not going to the freaking station!" Bobby took a step back and bumped into Andy. "Him neither. Go ahead. Arrest us."

"I'm pretty sure you don't mean that, son. Let's go cool off and that will be the end of it."

"It's the end of it right now. I'm not going anywhere."

Some spit flew out of Bobby's mouth. Donna saw the same face Bobby used to make when they still lived with their dad back in Ohio.

"Make me."

"Take it easy, officers. We don't want trouble."

Andy stepped in front of Bobby, but too close to the chief and bumped his chest and knocked him back a bit.

"That's it. You're both under arrest. Drunk and disorderly."

In a flash, Bobby and Andy were cuffed and escorted toward the police car. The rest of the party goers either gaped at the scene or scurried off. One of the police officers called out.

"Someone better call their parents."

The doors to the police cars slammed and their flashing lights whirled and the police car drove off and its siren blared.

"My mom's gonna kill Bobby." Donna ran into the kitchen to use the phone. "I'll call Andy's mom, too."

Tim watched her grab the phone and make the call. The party broke up and he found himself standing alone in the front yard. It was littered with beer cans and bottles of vodka. Everything he knew about the team and what happened to Bobby and Andy and Tim's own dad and his rules and how things had gone so terribly wrong made him feel sick. He bent over and his stomach wretched and he dry heaved since there wasn't anything inside him to throw up. Donna came out and rushed to Tim and tried to hold him up, but Tim wretched again and it sounded like a wounded animal from deep in the forest.

Chapter 49

A Time to Lose

News of the arrest shook the town and the team. When Coach Joe got a call at his house from the police, he answered calmly.

"I understand. Thank you for the courtesy, officer. I'll take care of it."

Coach Joe threw kids off the team in the past for drinking or doing drugs. But he had never thrown off a captain. Not for anything.

And then the thought came to him. What about his son? Did his son know about all the drinking, the drugs, the partying? He slowly sank into a chair. He felt terribly tired once again and he turned off the light in his living room and sat in the dark and tried to figure things out.

Mary Jones picked up her son at the police station. They drove home in silence. When they got into their driveway, Mary turned off the ignition. She looked out the windshield and waited for her son to talk. It took some time before Andy said anything.

"I'm sorry you had to come pick me up."

"I swear, Andy, I'm glad it was me and not your father."

"Jesus, mom. I know. But he isn't here and you had to do the dirty work."

"That's no fair, Andy, and you know it. Your dad loved you and I know you miss him, but he would have been just as upset at you as I am right now. You've embarrassed me. It wasn't like this before. And I think Bobby has everything to do with it."

"It's not just him. I could have said no to him, but something stopped me. The next thing I knew, I was drinking too much and even smoking dope and I couldn't seem to break away from him."

"You've always had Tim. Why didn't you reach out to him?"

"Mom, I did something awful to Tim."

"What did you do?"

"Me and Bobby. We told Tim we were going to party this season and we told him to keep quiet about it."

"Wait, what? Didn't you stop and think what you were doing to Tim? Didn't you see how he couldn't possibly do anything about what you and Bobby were doing?

"I guess I didn't think. I was so caught up in Bobby, and to be honest, I was caught up in the booze and the dope."

"Well, this isn't going to end well for you or Bobby or Tim. You know that, right? And you know this is going to get around and you know you've put Tim and Coach Joe in an awful situation. I really can't believe you did this. You're going to have to deal with the consequences. That's what your dad would say if he was sitting in this car today instead of me."

Andy sat for a while and then reached for the door handle and opened up the door and swung one leg out of the car. He still smelled of booze and dope.

"I know, mom."

He slid out of the car and closed the door behind him and walked up the steps to his house. Mary Jones sat in the car and wished for the millionth time her husband was still alive.

Donna and Bobby unlocked the door to their house and walked inside. Gwen Wilson sat in the kitchen with a cup of coffee in her hand. She didn't look at either one of her children. Donna put her car keys on the hook on the wall and kissed her mother and walked off to her room and left her mom and Bobby alone.

"Don't say anything, mom. Not one thing."

Bobby sat down across from his mother.

"No, this time you're going to listen, for God's sake. I've been through a lot with you and your sister, and I brought you out here because I thought it would be good for us and we'd be safe and you'd heal, but you haven't, and to be honest, I'm sick of it. You act like it was only you that got beaten by your dad. I have scars on my arms and neck and back and they're finally healing, but every time you screw up, it's like I'm bleeding all over again. For Christ's sakes, Bobby, will you just let your father go because I can't let it go until you do."

"You won't ever understand, mom. You can't understand what it was like to have to beat the crap out of dad and how, if the cops didn't pull me off, I would have killed him."

"Bobby, he's not your dad anymore and he's not my husband anymore. When we ran away, we did it because he was going to kill us. I've done the best I could to help you through all of this, and every time I think things are getting better, you screw up and rip our wounds wide open again. And you're not being the kind of man Coach Joe wanted you to be when he made you captain. I begged you to accept his offer and you gave your word that you would follow his rules. You lied to him, Bobby. Do you think he's not going to do anything about what you and Andy have done?"

"I don't care what he does. I'm the captain of the team and right now that's all the matters and he can't take that away from me."

"Well, he's a good man and he had faith in you. But he's the coach of the team and he has his rules and I know him just well enough to know he isn't going to let this pass."

"I don't care what he does to me."

"I know you don't care, Bobby. That's what disappoints me the most."

Chapter 50

Choice Lies

An emergency team meeting was called by Coach Joe for Monday before school. The team filed into the classroom next to Coach Joe's office. No one spoke. No one looked at Bobby or Andy when the two entered the room. Tim followed behind them. Not many looked at him, either.

"Gentlemen. A team rule has been broken. I've thought about it. Bobby and Andy should be dismissed from the team. But they're your captains. I think they should decide what should be done." The silence in the room was painful. It was a number of minutes before anyone spoke. Then Ike stood.

"I'd like to hear what Tim has to say about it."

As one, the team turned to look at Tim. All the assistants adjusted their desk chairs. Coach Joe sat at his desk. A lone bead of moisture formed on his forehead.

Tim sat motionless. It felt like a vice tightened around his chest. The team knew Tim knew about the parties and the drinking and the drugs.

"I don't have anything to say." Tim felt laser beams pierce his skull. A heavy rain began outside. "I really don't."

Ike looked at Tim and so did Jeff and the assistant coaches and the rest of the team. Tim felt weak in his chair, but didn't say the thing that should have been said about what Bobby and Andy did to him at the beginning of the season. Coach Joe saw the stillness of his team and coaches and his son. He waited some more and then he stood up and spoke.

"Well. Gentlemen, I've given this quite a bit of thought over the weekend. Actually, it's all I have been able to think about." He looked at his son. There was a flash to Coach Joe's stare. "I have decided that since Bobby and Andy are your captains, I will give them a say in their own consequence. We have a game against Billerica Friday night. They're undefeated and probably headed to the state playoffs. I don't have to tell you how big a game this is for you and the town."

Coach Joe waited a moment for the team and the assistant coaches to digest it all.

"That being said, Bobby and Andy, here are your choices. You can give up being captains and play Friday night against Billerica, or you can keep being captains and sit out the game." The depth of the choices slowly seeped into the brains of everyone on the team. "Bobby and Andy, do you understand the choices you have before you?"

"Yes, sir."

"Well, take some time in the hallway to think it through. Come in when you're ready. We'll wait here until you make your decision."

Bobby and Andy got up from their desk chairs. The legs of the chairs made a brutal screech as Bobby and Andy pushed them back.

The two were outside for a long time. The team could not hear what was being said. They didn't know if the two were even speaking. Finally, the door opened slowly. Bobby and Andy walked in and stood before their team. Andy spoke first.

"I've let you down. All of you. And especially you, Coach. You've been there for me though everything, and you helped my mother and my brothers when my dad passed. What I've done is unforgivable. I've decided I don't deserve to be a captain. But I don't want to make it worse. I want to play Friday night. Please, Coach. Don't change your mind."

Coach Joe looked at Andy.

"Very well. If that's your decision. Go take your seat."

Andy moved back to the empty chair. He tried to sit up straight, but his head bowed under the weight of all the choices he made since Bobby moved into town. The team exhaled and the rain let up a little outside.

"Bobby?"

All heads looked back up. Bobby thrust his hands deep into his jean pockets. He stared toward the back of the room and his eyes fixed on the wall.

"I'm not playing." Coach Joe looked hard at Bobby. "I'm staying captain."

The team sat in shock. Tim's legs felt paralyzed.

"And that's your decision? Are you sure, son?" Coach Joe leaned forward on his elbows.

"I have to be captain."

And at that moment, everyone in the room understood that he no longer was.

Andy looked up at Bobby. They said nothing to each other in the hallway. The moment Coach Joe gave him the choices, Andy knew exactly what he would do. He thought Bobby would do the same. Andy's jaw clenched. His vision blurred with anger and humiliation. Finally, Coach Joe broke the silence.

"Very well. It is done. Everyone, go to class. I'll see all of you at practice this afternoon."

Bobby moved quickly out the doorway and down the hall. The rest of the team followed. Andy walked pass Coach Joe but didn't look at him.

Tim remained seated in the desk chair. He felt drips of sweat soak the back of his shirt. His left hamstring ached. He got up stiffly and walked toward the door. His dad stopped him with a large hand on Tim's chest.

"Did you know about Bobby and Andy's drinking?"

The two faced each other. Tim looked at his dad and thought about Bobby and Andy and what they did to him when they cornered him. The team knew Tim went to the parties. He thought about how he felt broken inside and how he failed everyone but what came out of his mouth was a surprise.

"No. I did not know about the drinking, Coach."

For the first time in Tim's life, he lied to his father.

Practice that week was disjointed. Tim dropped easy passes from Jeff and Andy ran the ball without enthusiasm. Ike missed easy tackles and made half-hearted attempts at blocks. Bobby was relegated to the second team defense for the week. He chased running backs listlessly. When there was a water break, his teammates ignored him.

Coach Joe stood by himself on the sidelines. The week had worn on him as much as his team and he felt a tiredness that consumed him to his core. At one point, when the team took a water break, Coach Joe sat on a bench next to the practice field and tried to get in as many breaths as he could. He stood back up and resumed practice, and it took everything he had to keep going.

Chapter 51

Tired Eyes

On Thursday night, a day away from facing the undefeated Billerica Titans, Donna stopped by for pizza with Tim and Coach Joe. Tim showered upstairs and the pizza arrived. Coach Joe and Donna set out paper plates and soda cans. They sat in their customary chairs with Coach Joe at the head of the table.

"You're not right, Coach."

"I'm fine. Hand me a slice." Coach Joe deflected.

"I watch you during games and after my practices. You haven't been right since the Pentucket fight."

"I might be a little tired."

"You're more than tired, Coach." She reached out and put her hand on top of Coach Joe's. "It's been a tough week. It's been a tough year."

Coach Joe kept his eyes down. He looked up after a few seconds.

"What about you, Donna? How's it been at home?"

Coach Joe did not move his hand. Hers was warm. This was the first time in weeks that Coach Joe felt a little less tired.

"It isn't good. My mom comes home from work. I make dinner, or she does. Bobby takes his plate and eats in his room. He's not talking to us."

Coach Joe looked at Donna.

"No one is talking to him at practice."

Coach Joe moved his hand away and drank some soda. He had no appetite.

"I gave him a choice."

"Yes."

"It was the best I could do."

"Yes."

Tim came down stairs. He sat next to Donna opposite from his father. He took two slices and popped open a can of grape soda.

"And how are you, my fine young man?"

She put her arm through Tim's. Tim kept his head down and ate a small bite of pizza.

"I'm ready for Billerica."

Donna knew it was a lie. She watched football practices when her soccer team was done. She saw Andy flail about the field. She saw Ike stumble when he tried to make catches. She saw Tim drop easy passes from Jeff. She saw Coach Joe by himself with his eyes lowered. And she saw her brother, completely and utterly alone. He was an empty egg shell.

"Yes. I'm sure you are."

And they sat silently and ate cold pizza.

Chapter 52

For the Ages

The game was a disaster. Billerica scored at will against the lifeless Warriors. Tim was stripped of the ball on one of his runs and the Billerica defender waltzed into the end zone with the recovered fumble. Jeff had two passes picked off, one for a Titan score. Ike was a zombie. He ran awful routes and missed tackles. Only Andy seemed to have any energy. Still, he couldn't do it alone. The score at halftime was 35-0, Billerica. The rout was on.

Coach Joe stood outside the locker room. He felt a deep tiredness that he could not shake. He tried to think of a way to rally the team and avoid an embarrassing loss. His teams never lost like this. He hoped he could help them keep their dignity. He reached for the locker room door to make his way inside. He met Andy Jones's stare. Andy grabbed the door handle and pulled it shut with Coach Joe left outside. Andy jumped up on a bench in the locker room and ripped off his helmet and slammed it into a locker. The sound reverberated around the room and snapped the listless team to attention.

"I don't give a crap about winning this game, but I'm not losing this way. No freaking way."

He slammed his helmet into the locker again and put a big dent in it. He took his helmet and pulled it hard over his forehead and back onto his head. He jumped off the bench and grabbed the locker room door handle and flung it open and raced out and sprinted toward the field. Coach Joe froze when Andy ran past. So did the assistant coaches.

Tim watched his friend leap out of the locker room. He grabbed his helmet and sprinted after him. When they saw first Andy and then Tim storm out of the locker room, the whole team sprinted after them. They left Coach Joe and the assistant coaches to wonder what the hell just happened.

On the opening kickoff of the second half, the Billerica kicker sent a deep ball toward the sideline. Normally, Tim returned kicks, but this ball was too wide. The ball fell toward Ike. He gathered it up and ran toward the charging Titans. Four Titans swarmed toward him. Within a split second, one of them was sent hurtling into the Billerica cheerleaders. Andy raced across field and simply eliminated the Billerica kid. He pivoted immediately and blasted a second Titan. And then a third. He screamed as the last one somersaulted into the Billerica coaching staff.

Tim had not been idle. As he ran toward Ike to protect him from being wiped out, he saw the devastating blocks thrown by Andy. He heard Andy's maniacal scream. A hot fever took hold of Tim. A massive Titan took aim at Ike. Tim went airborne and leveled the Billerica lineman. Ike stiff armed another Titan and raced down the sideline. He was pulled down by two chasing Billerica players. The crowd screamed and cheered and couldn't quite believe what they saw. The fuse of the bomb was lit.

The Beaumont players pounded each other on the sideline, and the offense raced onto the field. Jeff took a quick snap and tossed the ball to Andy. Tim and Ike destroyed the Billerica cornerback. They crashed on top of him and knocked the wind loudly from his lungs. Instead of trying to avoid the Billerica safety, Ike took aim and lowered his helmet and shoulder pads and drove the Billerica player on to his back and Ike ran up and over the kid's chest. He stumbled over on his own momentum, but only after a 30-yard gain. Beaumont had the ball on Billerica's eight-yard line.

On the very next play, Coach Joe sent in a quarterback draw. On this play, Andy and Tim lined up beside Jeff in shotgun formation. Ike came in motion. When he was level with the center and the ball was snapped, Ike turned up field to trap block the Billerica defensive tackle. His legs churned and he drove the Titan off the line of scrimmage. Tim and Andy double teamed a Billerica's best defensive player. He had no chance. Tim hit him low and Andy hit him high and the two of them pancaked the kid.

Jeff ran into the end zone untouched and held the ball aloft in triumph.

The Beaumont fans felt the charge in the air. The Jones boys had come home from college to support their little brother. They screamed for blood. Their mother, Mary, hollered for the Warriors to rip the kidneys out of the Titans. Some of the crowd turned in shock when they heard what Mary shouted, but then they turned back around and screamed for similar bodily injuries.

Donna stood by herself at the top of the stands. Her friends on the soccer team grabbed each other and screamed. But Donna stood quietly. She saw Bobby walk into the stadium through the back entrance. She saw his gold hair lit up by the game lights. He wore his Beaumont varsity jacket with a big "B" on one breast and his captain's "C" on the other. He stood by himself far down the Beaumont sideline near the end zone where Jeff just scored. Bobby kept his hands in his coat pockets when the Beaumont sideline erupted. Andy, Tim, Ike, and Jeff butted heads in the end zone in celebration. They turned to run back to the Warrior sideline and they slowed down when they saw Bobby. They all turned away from him as they ran past and Bobby stood the rest of the game by himself watching the game like a hollow tree.

For every mistake Beaumont made in the first half, Billerica made two in the second. Andy played like a blazing fire. He seemed to make every tackle, every big block, and every tough run. He played possessed. The Billerica players were championship quality, but they feared Andy Jones that night.

Tim caught two passes for touchdowns. Ike sacked the Billerica quarterback and jarred the ball loose. He picked it up, and after Andy body slammed a Titan, Ike raced in for six. Andy scored on two long runs and Ike caught another touchdown pass from Jeff. The Warriors now led, 42-35. Tim picked off a late Billerica pass and raced untouched, 60 yards for the final score. He crossed the end zone and wound up and spiked the ball. The impact seemed to make the end zone shake.   The Billerica sideline was crushed. Donna smiled for the first time in the game.

Beaumont scored the last 49 points of the game.

Chapter 53

A Win and a Loss

Andy was delirious after the game. It wasn't the craze of joy that the Beaumont players and fans seemed to see. Andy felt rage. It was the greatest comeback in the history of the Beaumont Warriors, yet Andy felt no satisfaction from the win. Bobby's betrayal of him and his team could not be erased by a win, no matter how dramatic. Such was the terrible aura around him that no one on the team or any of his friends or even his mother dared come near.

When the game ended, the Warriors ran off the field whooping and hollering and letting the thrill of the victory completely take over every ounce of their hearts. Bobby watched the team run off the field in one direction and he turned and walked off in the other and he buttoned up his varsity jacket and walked back to his car and drove off completely alone.

Once again, Coach Joe let the celebration envelop his players while he stood off to the side. He never experienced anything like it in his own playing days and certainly not as a coach. It was like some terrible, demonic outside force had pulsed into his team.

And he felt a great fatigue. To the fans long accustomed to the mannerisms of Coach Joe, it looked just like how he acted after other big wins. He wanted the moment to be about his players.

Donna Wilson looked down at Coach Joe and saw it differently. She looked at him and saw Coach Joe look more like an old man than a coach who just saw his team come from behind in epic fashion.

She walked down from the top of the bleachers. She stopped for a moment and gazed at the wild celebration by the Beaumont fans and players. Her heart soared for the Warriors, and at the same time, it broke for her brother, and for Andy, and for Tim. She knew there was no mending any of them.

"I've never seen a game like that."

Coach Joe slumped in his kitchen chair later after the game. He and Tim shared a sub Tim picked up after the game. Pages of stats and a can of film lay on the kitchen table. Some of the ketchup from his sub dripped. Coach Joe moved the papers away and dabbed off the spill and it left a dark red smudge on one of the papers. Tim ate his part of the sandwich and looked at his dad.

"Andy was unbelievable."

Tim took another bite and remembered one of Andy's tackles when two Billerica players tried to make a block and Andy tossed them aside like rag dolls. Tim remembered the thud of pads as Andy drove his helmet into the chest plate of another Billerica player. He remembered the sight as the kid flew out of bounds and slid across the Beaumont High School track.

"I've never seen anyone play with that kind of intensity. It was frightening."

He found that his father looked at him intently.

"You played well too, son. You always play well. I'm not sure I've taken the time to let you know what a fine player you are. And you're a fine captain. I'm proud of you."

"I don't think you should be very proud of me." Tim put his sandwich down and wiped his fingers and lips. "I could have done more this season."

"You've done everything for this team and me. I couldn't ask for a better captain, or son." Coach Joe reached over and put his hand on Tim's. "I love you son. I know it's been hard on you being my son and playing for me and not having a mother around."

"Yes."

"You did it the right way. All of it."

"Not all of it." He reached for his sandwich, but then put it back down. "You don't know all of it, dad."

He stood up and walked over to the sink and turned to face his father.

"I lied to you. I knew about Bobby and Andy and their drinking and the drugs. I saw them all the time and I didn't do anything about it. At the beginning of the season, they told me I had to keep my mouth shut. I didn't know what to do, so I didn't do anything. I just didn't have the courage to deal with it."

Coach Joe looked at Tim for a long time and he took a very deep breath and let it out slowly and finally spoke.

"That was hard for you. Too hard for any kid. I don't know what else you could have done. But I should have seen it, son. I knew something was not right with the team. I saw you guys struggle and I thought you could fight through it, so I let it all be."

He stood up and walked over to his son and put his arms around him and held him for a long time and then stepped away and looked at Tim.

"They broke your heart, Tim."

"They did."

Tim hung his head.

"I'm not talking just about Bobby and Andy. They broke your heart and your heart has always been broken over your mom. This is going to be tough on you for a long time, Tim."

"I know."

Tim's face was pulled tight from going through the season the way he had to go through it, and maybe even going through the years he had to go through living alone with his dad and knowing his mother was out there somewhere.

"Go find Donna. You two should celebrate tonight's win. That's all you should think about right now. We'll figure things out on Monday when we get the team back together. Go on, now. Get out of here or you'll see your old man crying. Go on."

Tim left and closed the door and did not see his father fall apart after the lights dimmed and his dad sat alone.

Chapter 54

True Life

"Can we park here and walk to the party?"

Tim sat next to Donna as she drove toward Ike's house.

"Yes, if you want. I could use a good walk."

Donna pulled the car over and turned off the ignition. She got out of the car and locked it. She and Tim walked on the side of the road toward the faint sound of music in the darkness. They held hands and said nothing as they slowly moved down the street. A car full of partiers drove by. They did not see Donna and Tim in the blackness of the side of the road.

"I want to talk about my brother."

She held his hand with more firmness.

"I don't want to talk about your brother." The two walked on. Tim spoke quietly. "He almost broke us and he almost broke the team."

"Yes. But he didn't. What you guys did tonight at the game. I don't have words for it." She took her hand away from his and put her arm around his shoulders. "How Andy played. How you played. I don't know. I couldn't breathe watching you guys play. You had every reason to get beaten tonight, but you didn't. Even with Bobby not playing."

She slowed them down. Tim pulled her closer. Their foreheads touched.

"I have to tell you about Bobby. And my dad. I should have told you a long time ago, but I didn't know how, or maybe I didn't want to tell you anything." She stood silently for a moment and finally went on. "My dad beat us, Tim. Bobby tried to stop him. We're alive today because my mother got us the hell away from him, but no one ever really survives that."

"Your dad beat you and your mom and Bobby?"

"Yes. We left him in Ohio. He doesn't know where we live. I hate the bastard. That's why Bobby's angry all the time."

Tears streamed down her cheeks. She tried to stop crying. Tim took his finger tips and brushed some of the tear drops from her face.

"Part of my brother still loves my dad. Even with the beatings, with the swinging of the belt. With the open and closed fists."

"I don't understand."

Tim stood back.

"I see it, Tim. When Bobby gets in fights. When he gives cheap shots in games. When he wouldn't give up his captaincy. He's just fighting back against someone who didn't love him, didn't love us."

Donna stood in the dark, framed by a lone street light.

"Then one day, Bobby almost killed him. My father came home from work. Something didn't go right at the plant. I met him at the door. I tried to say hello, but he shoved me hard against the stove. I was maybe twelve. My mom was cooking something. When I hit the stove, it knocked a frying pan through the air. It just missed me. But the noise set my dad off even more. My mother stepped in front of me, but it was too late. He kicked me. Then he kicked my mom. She tumbled backwards and hit her head against a chair. It flew backwards and slammed into the wall. My dad came on. He grabbed my mom by the hair and pulled her up, slapping her along the way. I tried to bite him, but he kicked me again. That's when Bobby came in the kitchen." Tim watched Donna strain to get the story out.

"Bobby grabbed my dad by the wrists and tried to wrench his hands out of my mother's hair. I remember my mom screaming. My dad took a swing at Bobby, but Bobby was too quick. He ducked as my dad's fist flew past. He was off balance and Bobby tackled him. They crashed into the kitchen table with Bobby on top. Bobby swung an elbow at my dad and it hit him in the nose and then the mouth. He hit him so many times. He kept saying, 'I'll kill you! I'll kill you.' I've never heard that kind of sound coming from anyone. It was horrible. I saw blood gush from my dad's mouth. A neighbor must have heard the fight because the cops showed up. It took three of them to pull Bobby off my dad. He rolled in his own blood on the floor and he just moaned and held his jaw. Bobby was twelve years old, and it scared the shit out of me to see him try to crush my dad's head."

"Jesus."

Donna began to sob and Tim did his best to hold her, but these were wails of anguish she held in for years. He let her cry until she was done crying.

"The cops took us to the police station and my mom told them the story of how my dad had been beating her for years, ever since he started having trouble at the factory. She told them that Bobby had tried to protect her and me and that was the first time he hit back at my dad. The police decided not to press charges against Bobby. But they arrested my dad when he woke up at the hospital and they threw him in the city jail, and as they threw him he told them he was going to kill us.

My mom got a restraining order on my dad right then. Our lawyer told us that most times restraining orders don't work. So we packed up some clothes and stuff we needed and that very same day we fled. My aunt bought us bus tickets. We stayed in Arizona for a few weeks, then we moved to California and we had no money until my mom found a job.

We kept in touch with our lawyer back in Ohio. She told us that when our dad got out of the hospital, he got in a fight with some guy at a bar. He hit the guy over the head with a beer bottle. He's in some jail near Cleveland. But my mom is still scared he might get out and try to find us so we packed up again and moved here because she read about a job here in Beaumont. She's still scared out of her mind. So am I. I think Bobby is too. He's never gotten over almost killing my dad. None of us have, but Bobby did what he did and we saw it all and it was terrible and now we're here and it's like a piece of Bobby is dead."

Tim gently took Donna's hand and they started to walk again. Her shoulders relaxed and she wiped the rest of the tears away from her face. Tim looked at her as they walked. She was beautiful. More beautiful than anything he had ever seen, even with tear streaks on her face and puffy eyes from crying. It wasn't the beauty of her hair or her face or her body. He saw the beauty of her strength. He felt stronger because of how strong she was. She stopped and looked at him.

"And I think it's time for you to forgive yourself about what's happened with the team and what's happened between you and your dad. None of what happened with you and Bobby and Andy was your fault. What were you supposed to do when they forced you to stay quiet about their partying? You had to keep it from your father. That was hard."

"I know, but I'd never lied to my dad before. Maybe if I stood up to your brother and Andy at the beginning of the season, none of this would have happened."

"No. You were broken all season. Your dad too, probably. Bobby, and my mom, Andy and his family. Even me. But it wasn't your fault. People break. We can't always save them. Maybe we can just fix them a little. But everything that's happened. You couldn't fix it. You have to know that."

She took his face in her hands and kissed him. At that moment, everything was gone: the cowardice, the lies, the hatred. It all disappeared as he kissed her back.

"You know I love you," Bobby whispered while his lips brushed against hers.

"Of course you do."

And she led him onto Ike's front yard and music blasted and kids partied.

Chapter 55

Letter Jacket

Bobby sat in his car not far from Ike's house. A mostly empty bottle of vodka lay on the passenger seat along with a bag of chips and an old cheeseburger wrapper. He felt hot and a fever in his mind took hold. His stomach churned as the combination of vodka and bad food sat in his gut. He watched kids arrive at the party and he saw some of the guys on the team. They high fived and hugged and danced and drank and had the best time and he sat in his car and hated them all and he hated himself even more. Some of the left-over bits of fries rested on his letter jacket. The captain's "C" stunk of booze and there was still puke from parties days before. The fabric of his jacket still carried a slight smell of smoke from a night and a fire a couple years ago. Thoughts and images raced through his mind. Moving from town to town. Joining a new team. Celebrating over Andy's broken ankle. Recovering a fumble at states. Starting a fire in an empty house. Getting pulled out. Saving Andy. Getting a letter jacket. Seeing Daniel quit. Losing for the first time. Making captain. Cornering Tim about partying. Getting drunk and high way too much. Being arrested. Keeping his captaincy. Quitting on his team. Beating his dad when he was twelve and just a little boy.

He put on his letter jacket and tried to wipe off some of the old vomit. He stumbled out of the car, but reached back in to grab the vodka bottle. He walked into the party with the bottle grasped in one of his hands. Kids were everywhere and they looked at him without looking, the way high school kids can do. He took another swig of vodka and threw the empty bottle into the woods. He walked over to a keg and poured a beer. He looked around and saw Jeff Tony and Ike and Tim and Donna and cheerleaders and a victory cake and Andy. Andy stood against a brick fence by himself. Someone brought a cake and it was half eaten and Bobby saw Andy stick his finger in the frosting and lick it off. Bobby watched Andy look around the party. Bobby stood by himself with a beer in his hand.

Andy felt his blood get very warm and his eyes blur as the bass beat from the speakers pounded. His hands rubbed against a big vein that bulged in his neck. He had a water bottle in his hand and he dropped it and blindly strode towards Bobby. Kids moved aside. They felt a tangible, electric pulse that made them move out of the way.

Tim saw Bobby arrive at the party before Donna did. Donna talked to some friends and did not see her brother walk in and pour himself a beer. Tim felt the same pulse everyone else felt. His stomach churned and felt like he was going to throw up. A deep instinct made him walk away from Donna without telling her he was doing so. He headed straight toward the keg and the cake and the point where Bobby and Andy were about to meet. Donna turned away from her friends and expected Tim to be by her side, but then she saw her brother and Andy and Tim walking quickly toward them and Donna knew it was all very bad. She pushed pass some kids and caught up to Tim.

"The hell you doing here?" Andy's eyes blazed.

Tim saw the rage in his friend and he tried to get closer. Someone turned off the music.

"I can't be at a party? Shit."

"You quit on us, so I don't want you here. None of us want you here."

Andy shoved Bobby and he lost his balance and stumbled backwards. Bobby felt the stares and the disappointment and the humiliation and the loss of everything he thought he had. It was too much. He snapped and drove into Andy and the two fought on the grass. Bobby was on top of Andy and drove elbows into his face. Donna raced over and grabbed her brother, but he threw her off and kept elbowing Andy. Andy drove a knee into Bobby's ribs and pushed him off and then shoved him against the rock wall and beat him in the face with his fists. Andy grabbed Bobby's letter jacket and ripped it off and threw it in the woods. He threw a punch and it hit Bobby square in the jaw and knocked him back into the table with the cake on it. Bobby crashed over the table and the cake exploded and he was covered by it as he sprawled on the ground. The sudden crash made everyone laugh, but at that moment, a piece of Bobby's mind snapped. The cake knife was there and Bobby was insane, and he grabbed it and leaped up and drove the steely knife into Andy's chest. Andy's eyes widened and he pulled himself away and fell back off the knife and Tim was there and he caught him and the two dropped back to the ground. Andy let out a blood-curdling scream.

"I don't want to die! I don't want to die!" He writhed in Tim's arms and his legs kicked out and he begged Tim not to let him go. "Hold on to me. Dear God, Tim, hold on to me."

Tim cradled Andy's head and then felt blood all over his own hands as it gushed from Andy's chest.

"No, Bobby!" Donna charged her brother and slammed him backwards. She jumped on his chest and slapped his face. "You killed him!"

She saw only black, lifeless eyes when she looked down at her brother. He pushed her off and got up and looked down and saw Tim holding Andy. Bobby looked at his right hand and he saw the knife and the blood. His hand shook and he dropped the knife on the ground and he looked around and everyone stared at him but no one moved. Bobby turned and ran to his car and gunned it and flew off and swerved down the road and raced away. He drove hard into the night.

"I got you. I'm here. I won't let you go." Tim took off his hoodie and pressed it down against Andy's chest. It hurt and Andy screamed and tried to wrestle free, but Tim held him down. "I know, Andy. I know it hurts. I have to press down. I'm sorry." His hoodie was red from Andy's blood, but Tim kept up the pressure. The police arrived followed by an ambulance. When they got there, a police officer told Tim to move away. An EMT kneeled down and peeled off Tim's blood-soaked hoodie. He replaced it with thick bandages and pressed down on the wound.

"Tim. Tim! Tim. I'm scared. Jesus, it hurts."

Tim sat behind Andy and held him as partiers looked on and the EMT's tried to stop the blood.

Donna ran back. Some of her friends tried to hold her, but she pushed them away and kneeled down next to Andy and stroked his hair. He looked up at Donna.

"I know Bobby didn't mean it." Andy cried. "He was so angry. He didn't mean it."

"Please help him." Donna pleaded with the EMTs and she leaned over and kissed Andy's forehead.

The police cleared a path for the EMT's to take Andy away. They put him on a stretcher and wheeled him toward the ambulance. Donna and Tim followed with Jeff and Ike right behind. An EMT spoke quietly to Tim and Donna.

"Another inch and the knife would have pierced his heart. You got the bleeding stopped and that was key. I think he'll be ok." The news jolted Tim. He thought his friend was about to die. He fell into Donna's arms, and Ike and Jeff joined them.

Andy was loaded into the ambulance. Donna spoke softly to him.

"You'll be ok."

She looked deep into his eyes.

"It wasn't your brother's fault," Andy said and the ambulance door closed.

Donna pulled Tim's hand and the two ran to her car.

"We have to find Bobby!"

They jumped in and Donna raced down the road in the direction Bobby fled. The windows in the car fogged in the freezing air.

Donna pushed hard on the gas pedal and her car blew through a stop sign and sped down the road.

"We'll find him."

Tim put both hands on the dashboard as Donna's car hit 90.

Chapter 56

Fireballs

Bobby gunned the engine and flew down a back road. He didn't know which one. The steering wheel had blood on it. His gold hair flew from air flying in from the open sun roof on the top of his car. His mind squirmed. He just killed his best friend. This was the second time he held death in his hands. This time, no one stopped him. He wailed in anguish as his car took a small rise and the road bent sharply to the left. He yanked hard on the steering wheel, but it was too late. His car heaved to the right and gyrated wildly. The glass in the front window shattered when it first landed on its side and then the car flipped again and again and Bobby's body was flung out of the sun roof before the car finally came to rest in a field near some woods. The car wheezed and smoked like the life was slowly seeping out of it. A spark lit and the spilled gas ignited and the car burst into flames.

Bobby crashed end over end and came to a sudden stop near an old wire fence. Both his legs were turned at bad angles and he felt a searing pain in his right arm. He tried to roll over to grab onto his arm and saw that it was gone and blood was everywhere and he looked back and saw his car explode and thought that maybe all of his pain was finally over.

Donna kept her foot hard on the accelerator. Tim looked through the iced-up windshield. He searched for tail lights. Both of them saw a fireball rise in the distance.

"Jesus."

Tim leaned forward and peered over the dashtop. The car jumped the rise and almost crashed where the road turned. Donna slammed on the brakes and the car spun out but regained its balance so it didn't flip. She jumped out of her car and ran toward the woods and the fire and screamed for her brother because he was in the car. Tim raced after her.

"Bobby! Oh my God! Bobby. Jesus, Tim. Bobby's in there. We have to get him out!"

She pulled her shirt up over her mouth and face and tried to get close, but the flames melted the glass of the car and the chassis collapsed and Donna was sure to get burned so Tim pulled her away.

"Let me go! Oh, my God, my God, my God! My God! My God!" and Tim held her and cried with her and it was all too much for the both of them. "My God, My God. He can't die!" She moaned and Tim turned her away from the flames.

He saw a cop car race down the road. It slammed to a stop and two cops got out and they had a fire extinguisher and they rushed to put out the fire.

"Save him! Save him, my God, save him!"

She tried to break from Tim, but he pulled her back. One of the cops got closer to the car and tried to look inside. He covered his face with his forearm.

"I don't see anyone. I don't think anyone's in there!"

The other officer shut off his extinguisher and moved closer to his partner.

"Are you sure? Lord, then let's look around. The body must have flown out of the car. Be careful. I can't see a thing."

The two officers turned on their flashlights and searched near the car. They were blinded by the fire and it was hard for their eyes to adjust to the dark.

Donna pushed Tim away and screamed for her brother. She ran toward the trees. Tim raced in the other direction and tried to peer through the dark.

"Help. Help. I need help."

Tim heard a low whimper. Her turned toward that quiet sound and he saw Bobby lying against the wire fence. Tim shouted over the roar of the flames.

"He's here. Jesus, he's alive! I don't believe it! Help me! He's alive."

The two officers ran to the sound of Tim's voice and nearly tripped over Tim and Bobby. Donna hurtled an old stump and slid to a stop where Tim held Bobby. The ground was sticky with blood. Bobby's eyes looked small.

"I killed him. I killed my friend." Bobby coughed. He tried to move his body and couldn't feel his legs. He felt nothing where his arm was supposed to be. "Let me die, my God, just let me die."

"No way, Bobby. You're not dying. You didn't kill Andy. He's alive. We left him with the EMT. He said Andy was going to be ok. He's going to be ok!"

Tim ripped off his shirt and balled it up and pushed it into the part of Bobby's arm where the blood spurted. Bobby screamed, but Tim pushed down and his shirt filled with Bobby's blood.

One of the police officers ran to the squad car and called for an ambulance. The other took out some gauze from the medical kit Donna retrieved from the police car. The officer asked Tim to move out of the way. He took a wad of gauze and pressed hard where Tim had just pressed. The other officer came back with an oxygen tank and water. He placed the oxygen mask on Bobby and washed blood off his face and hands. There were no burns anywhere that the officer could see. Bobby's face was swollen and there was a cut just above his eye, but it was a small cut and the police officer put a bandage on it. The officer put splints on Bobby's legs and wrapped them with thick bandages. They heard the wail of an ambulance. It pulled in and EMT's jumped out with a stretcher and orange med kits. A fire truck pulled up and firemen pulled out hoses and doused the fire that had incinerated the car. Bobby groaned. The pupils in his eyes were small and his breathing was labored.

"But I stabbed him. My God. But he's not dead? I didn't kill him?"

Donna kissed her brother's forehead and wiped some blood away from Bobby's mouth. Tim kneeled close.

"He's alive, Bobby. He said you didn't mean it. He told me that. It's ok. You're both ok."

The EMTs picked Bobby up and put him on the stretcher and ran with him out of the woods and put him in the ambulance.

"Everything hurts so much, Donna. I hurt bad. I almost killed him."

Bobby whispered in Donna's ear and the EMT's secured the stretcher in the ambulance and shut the door.

"I'll drive your car to the hospital."

Tim took the keys from Donna's hands. She turned to Tim.

"Thank you, Tim. Be careful."

And the ambulance drove off and Bobby passed out and Donna held him and the siren wailed and the road and hospital seemed too far away.

Chapter 57

Waiting Rooms

Mary Jones ran from her car and pushed pass a security guard at the entrance to the emergency room.

"Please tell me where my son is! Someone, please help me!" Mary looked frantically for her son in the crowded waiting area. A nurse rushed through a door and took Mary's hand.

"Mrs. Jones. Please come with me. He's down here."

The nurse wrapped an arm around Mary and punched a big, silver button. Two large doors swung open and the nurse helped Mary passed stretchers and waiting people and doctors and other nurses. The two stopped next to a big green curtain. The nurse pulled the curtain open and there were two nurses and two doctors who worked on Andy. The nurse touched a doctor's arm.

"Mrs. Jones is here."

The nurse let go of Mary. One of the doctors moved aside and there was Andy with his head rolled back and the emergency room cot covered with blood. Mary held her hands to her face. She leaned over her son and ran her fingers through his sweat-soaked hair. He opened his eyes.

"I'm ok." He coughed and it hurt and he groaned. He looked at his mother. "I'll be fine."

"My God, what happened, Andy?"

She could see bandages just below his left shoulder. She touched them instinctively. Andy gave out a whimper and Mary took her hand away. A doctor in green scrubs and a hair net gently took Mary's arm and led her outside the curtained area and sat down with her on a wooden bench not too far away.

"Mrs. Jones, my name is Dr. Drivas. Your son is going to be ok. The stab wound was deep, but the blade missed the heart by about two inches. Your son has lost a great deal of blood, so we're giving him a transfusion. But we got him to the hospital quickly. One of his friends saved him when he slowed down the bleeding. The kid stuffed his hoodie into your son's wound. They said his name was Tim."

Mary looked at the doctor. She was in shock and had a hard time understanding what the doctor told her.

"Someone stabbed him? Jesus, who?"

"There was a fight, Mrs. Jones. One of your son's friends got in a fight with your son and stabbed him. That's all I know. The police will be able to tell you more. The good thing is your son is alert and the wound will heal in time. Your son is lucky he's alive. Now, I have to go and help him. Give me some time with Andy and we'll come get you as soon as you can see him."

Mary stood up from the cold, wooden bench with the doctor and he put his hand on her shoulder.

"He'll be fine. Why don't you wait and rest in the waiting room down the hallway? I'll have someone walk you down. Can someone please take Mrs. Jones to the waiting area?"

A very big man with a beard came over and took Mary's arm and led her down the hallway. They had to go out through the ER entrance. Another ambulance pulled in and the EMTs got out and ran around to the back and pulled out a stretcher. A doctor and two more nurses pushed pass Mary. They got to the stretcher and pushed it quickly down the corridor. The big man with the beard moved Mary away from the doctors and nurses. He helped her through the automatic doors and walked her to a small waiting room. A TV played something and a couple people sat in chairs and stared at it. Mary sat and the big man asked if she wanted to call someone and she said she did and he brought her a phone and she called Zeke and Alex and Coach Joe and told them what happened. They said they were on their way and she hung up and watched the TV without focusing and Mary Jones felt the world spin beyond her reach.

"We need to get this man to surgery. Call up to let them know we're on our way."

A doctor gave quick orders and the medical staff rushed Bobby toward a green elevator and Donna tried to follow. Her face was flushed and it was hard for her to swallow. She reached to hold Bobby's hand but there was no arm on that side of his body. A nurse put her hands onto Donna's shoulders.

"Sweetie, we're going to need you to go to the waiting room. We'll do everything we can for your brother. Do you want to call anyone?"

They found her a phone and she called her mother, but she didn't pick up. Donna hoped someone called her already.

A big man with a beard appeared and took Donna's hands and led her back through the ER just as her mother ran in.

"Tell me he's alive, Donna!"

"He's in the operating room. He's hurt bad mom."

"God! Tell me what happened."

And Donna told her everything about the game and the party and the fight and the knife and the crash and how Tim found Bobby and kept him from bleeding out. Gwen's legs gave out and she sagged to the floor. The big man with the beard helped Donna pick up her mom. He spoke gently to Gwen.

"Let me take you both to a waiting room down the hall."

He put a large arm around Gwen's shoulders and he and Donna helped her down the hallway and there was a waiting room and he opened the door for them. He stepped aside to let them in, and Donna and Gwen saw Mary Jones. The three looked at each other and tears burst from them all and they tried to hold on to each other as the universe began to disappear.

A team of doctors worked on Bobby's arm while another team worked on his legs. A doctor carefully unwrapped the bandages from Bobby's shoulder just above where his arm used to be. He cleaned the wound. He took very fine thread and stitched the stump and wrapped it with clean bandages. He moved over to where the other team worked on Bobby's legs. They were badly broken. They brought in a portable x-ray machine and took pictures and decided what had to be done. They operated on Bobby and put pins in both legs and wrapped them in plaster and put Bobby on a rolling hospital bed. Two of the doctors walked along and they transferred Bobby to the ICU. They helped two nurses lift him onto the bed and attach his legs to wires that hung from a silver metal frame. Bobby started to wake up and he began to moan, so they gave him more pain killers and he fell asleep again. The nurses hooked him up to a heart monitor and gave him oxygen. He lost a great deal of blood, but he seemed strong and they said to each other that they thought he would make it. One of the nurses went to find Donna and Gwen. As she left the room, she dimmed the light just a bit, and Bobby lay on the hospital bed and medical machines beeped and the I.V. dripped.

Coach Joe sat with Mary and Tim in Andy's room. Andy stirred and tried to sit up, but Mary placed her hand on his shoulder and eased him back onto the bed.

"Where's Bobby?" Andy looked first at his mom's face and then to Coach Joe's. "I need to speak with him."

Mary bent down so her face was inches from Andy's.

"He's at the other end of the hallway."

She took a damp facecloth and wiped his mouth.

"He crashed his car after he stabbed you. His legs are badly broken, Andy. He lost his right arm. He's in bad shape."

Mary's eyes remained focused on her son.

"Where am I?"

He looked around and felt confused for a long time, and then his eyes came into focus and the memory rushed back of the game and the party and the fight and Bobby. He remembered the cold knife and how Tim caught him when he fell.

"Am I alright?" Andy winced and felt a dull ache just below his left shoulder. He moved a hand to touch it and felt a thick bandage. "Is Bobby going to die?"

"Let's just worry about you, shall we, Andy."

"No, tell me about Bobby."

"His doctor's say they think he's going to be ok."

The pain medicine wore off and Andy groaned and Tim went to get a nurse. She came in and put a needle into Andy's I.V. bag and in a few moments the meds kicked in and Andy murmured Bobby's name and slowly fell back to sleep.

When they brought Bobby in after the surgery, the doctor told Gwen and Donna the surgery had gone well. His legs would heal and the doctor said he was sure Bobby would walk again. They cleaned the place where Bobby's arm used to be, and they didn't see any signs of infection, but they would have to keep a close eye on that. Gwen thanked the doctor and he left the room. They watched over Bobby and pulled chairs over and tried to rest. Both finally fell into a fitful sleep. They woke any time Bobby stirred. A nurse came in every few minutes and checked on him. She looked carefully at the amount of pain meds still in the I.V. drip. She checked the bandages on his arm and shoulder and adjusted the pillows under his legs and just before she left, Bobby woke up. His eyes moved around the room and he tried to focus them. He didn't know where he was or how he got here and why his mom and sister were asleep in chairs.

"There you are. How do you feel?"

The nurse put a blood pressure sleeve on Bobby's remaining arm. Gwen and Donna got out of their chairs and leaned over Bobby and kissed him and put their hands on his chest and felt his heart and tried not to cry.

"Jesus." Bobby took a deep breath and his legs hurt and he let out a cry. "Help me. My legs. Jesus, they hurt!" Bobby rolled to his side and he saw the bandages where his arm should have been. It took him a few moments for the information to make sense to his brain, and when it finally did, he screamed out, "Where's my arm? What happened to my arm?"

Bobby thrashed in the hospital bed and Donna tried to hold him down. She made gentle coyote noises like the ones from the desert back in Bakersfield a lifetime ago. She cradled his head in her arm and stroked his forehead and he began to calm down a bit. Gwen lay her head down on Bobby's pillows so she could be as close to him as she could get. Finally, Gwen sat back up and looked at her son.

"You lost your arm when the car flipped and you flew out. Tim found you and he saved your life. He stopped the bleeding from your arm until the EMTs could get you to a hospital."

Gwen took Bobby's face in her hands.

"You're going to be fine, Bobby. Try not to move. I know it hurts. You're not dying and we're going to be here and we're going to help you. My God. I love you, my dear, sweet boy."

Bobby looked into his mother's eyes. The pain was bad and he let out a whimper and he started to thrash about again. Gwen jumped up and called for the nurse.

"Can you please give him something? He's in so much pain!" The nurse came back into the room and she put a syringe into the I.V. bag that hung above Bobby. The drug dripped into the clear plastic. Bobby's body began to relax and Donna took a wet cloth and placed it on Bobby's forehead. He tried to talk, but it was hard for Donna and Gwen to hear him. They leaned closer.

"I killed him."

Bobby tilted his head back. Tears rolled down his cheeks. Gwen kissed him.

"No, Bobby. You didn't kill him. He's ok. You're both going to be ok." Gwen looked into Bobby's blue eyes and ran her fingers through his gold hair. "He's alive. He's in a room down the hall with his mom and Tim and Coach Joe."

"But I stabbed him! My, God, I stabbed Andy."

He tried to raise his voice but the drugs began to work and he started to doze off. Donna spoke calmly to her twin brother.

"Just close your eyes and go back to sleep. We'll be here when you wake up. Just rest now."

And Bobby closed his eyes and slept for a long time and the sun came up and the room brightened and Donna and Gwen tried to stay awake but they couldn't and the nurses and doctors came and went and let the two women sleep.

Chapter 58

Pizza for All

Donna and Mary and Tim and Coach Joe sat in Andy's room. The doctor told Mary that Andy would probably be able to go home in a few days. The wound was beginning to heal and there was no sign of infection. Mary stood up from her chair and walked over to where Tim sat. She took his hands and pulled him up and looked at him. Finally, she kissed his cheek and pulled him close and held him very tightly. After a while, she loosened her hug and stepped back a bit but still held his hands.

"I slapped you the night of the fire. I was so angry at Andy and at you and at everyone and at my husband for dying. I slapped you because I had no one else to slap. My God, Tim. You saved my boy the other night. He's loved you like a brother since the day he met you. And I hit you and you haven't come to visit us since, and that was two years ago. I'm so sorry. Thank you for holding on to my son and not letting him go."

She kissed him again. Tim's eyes were moist and he smiled at her and realized how much he missed her.

"He's my friend, and he'll be that forever, Mrs. Jones."

"Jesus, Ma. You're going to make him cry."

Andy laughed and sat up in his bed and took a plate of Jell-O from the hospital tray and held it out for Tim.

"Want some? I mean, you did save my life. Look. I saved you the last bite."

He held it up and wiggled it so the red goop and the leftover whipped cream shimmied. Mary laughed and so did Tim and so did Andy, but it hurt a bit. He slurped the last of the Jell-O and lay back down.

The door opened and Zeke and Alex walked in. They were followed by Steve Staber and Bill Bradner and Ike and Jeff Tony. Daniel Russell followed a few steps behind. Coach Joe saw Daniel and stood up and took a few steps forward and put his hand out. Daniel took it. They looked at each other for the first time in a long time. Coach Joe spoke first.

"I'm glad you're here."

Daniel held Coach Joe's grip.

"Me too, Coach."

"Are you ok, Daniel?"

"Yes, sir. I'm sorry, sir. I'm sorry for everything." Daniel looked around the room. His friends smiled. Daniel looked at Andy. "I'm glad you're going to be ok, Andy."

The room was quiet. Andy looked at Daniel.

"So am I," Andy laughed and extended his hand. Daniel took it and they shook hands warmly.

Mary watched while she stood with Tim. A tear rolled down her face. The door to Andy's room flew open.

"So what the hell is going on in here? Jesus, and no one brought pizza!"

Quick Lou Zarro burst into the room. He carried three enormous pizza containers.

"Hold these for me, will you Daniel."

He stuck the pizzas in Daniel's hands and walked to the bed and took Andy in a huge hug that made Andy laugh and wince at the same time.

"What the hell are you doing in here? Shouldn't you be getting ready for the next game?"

Quick Lou cried like a child and hugged his friend and wouldn't let go until a nurse came in and told everyone they were making too much noise. Andy let go of Quick Lou. He laughed and cried and said to the nurse, "What about the pizza?" The nurse smiled in spite of herself and said she would take care of the pizza, but everyone had to leave because visiting hours were over and Andy needed sleep. Everyone shuffled out of the room and Mary kissed her son's forehead and Quick Lou put his arms around Zeke and Alex and Tim and Ike and Donna and Daniel and they all left and the lights were dimmed and Andy rested.

Chapter 59

Open Doors

Late that night, the door to Bobby's room quietly opened. Andy stepped in and took a seat in a chair next to Bobby's bed. He looked at Bobby's broken legs and missing arm and a piece of Andy's heart broke and he cried silently. For a long time, Bobby remained asleep. Once in a while, a nurse came in to check on Bobby. She took care of Bobby and let Andy sit in the chair silently. He looked out the window. It was the darkest part of the night and he wondered if the sun might ever rise.

After a while, Bobby opened his eyes. The two looked at each other but didn't speak for quite a while. Finally, Andy broke the silence.

"I'm sorry."

"Why are you sorry? I almost killed you."

"But you didn't. I talked with Donna and your mom. They told me everything about you and your dad. Why didn't you tell me?"

"I never told anyone."

"That's a heavy weight to carry. Jesus, maybe I could have helped you. I think you almost told me about your dad once. It was the night you saved my life. The night of the fire sophomore year, the day we won states."

"And now you're here to make me feel guilty. I don't need your pity. Get the hell out of my room." Bobby shouted out, but Andy didn't budge. He looked hard at Bobby.

"You know what? You can stick that shit up your ass. I'm here because you don't deserve any of the shit you've gone through."

Andy moved his chair closer and put a hand on Bobby's chest. Bobby tried to squirm to the farthest part of the hospital bed, but he found he no extra room. Andy raised his voice a bit.

"We're both broken, and I can't heal without you. And it's time for you to let go of the ghost of your dad. The bastard had it coming. You didn't pick him for a dad. Neither did your sister, and your mother sure as hell wouldn't have picked him for a husband if she knew what he would turn into. Sometimes dads or moms don't deserve the kids they make. My dad's gone, and I can't get him back, but he was a good man and he loved me, and I'll hold on to him forever. Your dad was a prick and nothing he did to Donna or you or your mom was your fault and it's time you cut him loose. He doesn't deserve you."

"You think it's that simple?" Bobby shifted in his bed. Andy could see the bandages on Bobby's stump. "I lost my arm. My legs are busted. My mom doesn't deserve what I've put her through. Neither does Donna, or you, or Tim, or Coach Joe."

The silence lasted a long time. Andy said nothing but kept looking at his friend.

"I should have burned to death in that car."

Bobby closed his eyes hard. Andy pushed on Bobby's chest and it made him scream, but Andy kept pushing.

"But you're not dead. I think if you die in that car crash, your mom and Donna die too. And so do I. And every time I feel pain in my chest, after that I'll think of your stinking wasted life. Bullshit! You're too strong and you're too good and you didn't know what you were doing when you found the knife in your hand. Maybe if you did kill me you would have died in the crash. But you didn't kill me because you couldn't kill me. Something held you back."

Andy smiled and waited a moment to let what he said sink in.

"So just let it all go. Let go of the anger you've wrapped yourself in for all these years. It's like a stupid varsity captain's jacket. None of us really deserve wearing one. Let it go. Let what you think your dad should have been just all go. The hell with him!"

"That's all? Just say the hell with him and everything will be fine and fixed and perfect?" Bobby turned away from Andy. "You think you understand, but you never will."

"Well, screw that." Andy leaned closer. "I wasn't there with your dad when you were a kid, and you're right. I'll never understand, but you saved your mom and Donna. Do you hear what I'm telling you?" Andy got out of his chair and leaned over Bobby and grabbed him by the stump and held it tight and Bobby cried out, but Andy held on. "The only thing that matters at all is that you saved your mom and you saved Donna and the rest is all bullshit and it's over and you will let go of all of it. Do you hear me?"

Andy burst out crying and Bobby turned back to him and he started crying too.

"I don't know how to let it go."

"I'll help you, and so will your mom, and my mom, and Donna, and Tim, and Coach Joe."

"After everything I've done, you'll help? My God, Andy, how is that possible?

"I love you, my brother. I love you and Tim and Coach Joe, and your sister, and our moms. Our love should be enough. And it will be enough. Just let it in, Bobby. Let us all love you and just let it in." Bobby burst out a cry and his body shook in spite of the physical pain. He reached over to Andy with his one arm and his fingers opened wide and he grabbed onto Andy's hand. Andy pulled Bobby close and they wept in each other's arms and they couldn't stop and didn't stop for a very long time until finally the light of the morning slowly lit the room.

Chapter 60

The Light of Stars

The night after their graduation, Donna and Tim sat on a hillside overlooking Memorial Field. There were things that hadn't yet been said. It was a warm summer evening and clouds blotted out the light from the stars. The two held hands for a long time. Donna looked at Tim.

"I think Bobby and Andy are going to be ok."

"I do too. And your mom?"

"She's good. She and I help Bobby get around. He's walking almost without a limp. My mom sneaks into his room at night sometimes. She stares at him when he's sleeping. Sometimes I go in when she's in there. I watch his chest rise and fall and thank God you found him at the crash. He was talking about college the other day. He says he's not ready yet, but maybe next year. He's going to a therapist and he says it's helping. He told a joke the other day. That's the first joke he's ever told, at least for a very long time."

Tim tilted his head back.

"I was at Andy's yesterday. He told me the University of New Hampshire football coach wants him to play there. Andy told me the coach was at the Billerica game. Offered Andy a full ride. Told Andy he'd never seen anything like it. He called me and the other day we lifted weights and ran some sprints together. He's almost brand new."

Tim let out a deep breath and fireflies flew about. They were quiet for a long time. Donna put her hands behind her head.

"None of what any of us went through was fair. We found ourselves in a very dark thing and we couldn't stop it from happening. I don't know. Maybe it ruined all of us."

A breeze blew Donna's hair, so it covered her eyes. She brushed it back behind her ear.

"What about you? Are you ruined, Donna?"

He rolled over on his side to look at her. She lay there for a long time before she spoke.

"Maybe some part of all of us is ruined. There was too much pain and suffering and lying and hatred and violence, and it was a poison and it had to come out. How do any one of us really ever get over what we've been through?"

Tim looked at the pitch black of the cloudy night-time sky.

"I don't know, Donna. Maybe we won't ever get over this. But I know Bobby's better and I know Andy's better. I know my dad's taking some time off this summer to think coaching football and maybe what else he might try. The years have worn on him. I think he sees that now. I don't know."

He was quiet for a bit.

"And I'm finally thinking I'm ok knowing my mom's gone and it wasn't because of my dad or me. It was because of her. It's hard to admit, but I think that's the way it was supposed to turn out."

Tim took a deep breath.

"I think my dad is finally ok with just me and him. Maybe he'll take up the guitar or something."

"Coach Joe? Yeah. Right."

She giggled, and Tim touched her face with his fingertips. She held his hand tightly and she cried for the first time since she began to believe her brother was not going to die. After a while, her crying stopped, and she looked at Tim.

"We're both off to college and now you're going to lose me and I'm going to lose you." She pulled him closer. They breathed together. "Can you survive it?"

Her forehead rested against his. The night time breeze brushed over them.

"No, I don't think I can survive it. But I think we can survive it. I don't know me existing without you." He lay there. "But I think I know what we have to do."

"What's that?"

She pulled him over and pressed tightly against him.

"Just keep holding on. Maybe for right now and maybe forever."

The two of them lay beneath the darkness of the summer night and the stars came out just for them for the first time in a while.

ABOUT THE AUTHOR

Rick Collins is a teacher and coach of thousands of students and athletes from Penacook, New Hampshire, Andover, Massachusetts, and Plainville and Simsbury, Connecticut. He lives in Simsbury, Connecticut, with his adored wife, Betsy Dietlin Collins and is the loving father of his daughter, Hannah, and son Sam.

Rick Collins

49183570R00139

Made in the USA
Middletown, DE
18 June 2019